Rise from the Mud…Breathe

Phillip O'Donnell

To Rita who truly loves

To Alexander who let me be me

To Quinten who helped lay the foundation for it all

PROLOGUE

As Lucas walked through the central exam room, he saw Dr. Kevorkian and Kevin holding down a dog to administer an injection. He stopped for a moment to observe. As Dr. Kevorkian pulled back on the syringe, the dog's blood mixed with the pink solution inside. To Lucas, the dog looked cute and in a pleasant mood despite being at the veterinary clinic. He turned away for a couple of seconds, and when he looked back, he noticed the dog had gone completely limp with its tongue hanging out.

"Whoa!" he cried to Dr. Kevorkian. "One moment it was awake, and the next wasn't. That took me by surprise."

"Yes, the euthanizing agent acts quickly."

"I see."

Lucas hurried to the bathroom. As he turned on the water faucet and washed his face, he couldn't help mumbling "Just like that. One second alive, and the next not. Is this what our lives are: a flash of existence extinguished by another's hand?"

After drying off, he went about the rest of the day in deep contemplation of the transience of life. No one noticed the more somber expression on his face nor his absentmindedness. Maybe, he hid it well, or perhaps, the change was too subtle for anyone but him to notice.

When he arrived at home later that evening, he told his father "I think it's time for me to quit the animal clinic."

"Why? What happened?"

"These people don't seem to care about the deeper meanings of existence. They just focus on the day to day trying to survive. I'm bored, and I feel like I'm wasting my time." He explained.

"Well, do what you think is best."

Recently, Lucas had an epiphany that life should not be wasted on pursuing careers because they are conventional and safe, rather one should pursue one's dreams else suffer a miserable existence. No longer would he deny the expression of his hopes, passions, and dreams for the sake of conformity and normalcy. He pledged to live only for the adventure of becoming.

The animal clinic was the start of this endeavor, and the time for him to move on appeared to have arrived. He only accepted the position as a veterinarian technician assistant to learn about veterinary medicine, which as a child he imagined as one of many possible futures, but he never gave himself a chance to investigate the profession until now. He found this particular place to not suit his aspirations nor needs. Therefore, on to the next.

He sat down in his thinking chair and began to brain storm.

"What am I to do next? He asked aloud to himself. "Nothing seems quite right for me. Everything seems boring. Maybe, I'm looking at the wrong things."

He rose from his thinking chair and began writing on his white board. In big bold letters he wrote at the top *How Do I Find Myself?*. He, then, began filling the whiteboard with ideas. After he felt he had written all he could, he sat back in his thinking chair.

"No, none of this is any good!" he yelled.

He started erasing everything. This time he wrote on the top *Rise From The Mud!* He sat back down, and a smile slowly grew on his face.

"Yes, that's it. That has to be it!" he exclaimed.

THE SEARCH

Lucas walked underneath skyscrapers on the streets of downtown as he conducted research on the fundamental values of his city. Occasionally, he would stop to talk to those willing, asking about life. He asked them who they were and what they lived for. Things had become considerably desperate for him lately, so he decided to directly address those who perplexed him. Even though people received him and his questions well, each interaction left him feeling empty and wishing for more. People's answers seemed too plain and too boring to nourish him.

When he observed the downtown area from a skyscraper's sixtieth floor Sky Lobby earlier that morning, he glumly thought before him lies an empire of hollow values dedicated to exulting nothingness. At that moment, the loneliness he felt became a concrete reality, and discouragement overcame him. He began to doubt the usefulness of his pursuit and considered going home, but as he exited the building a wave of strength and purpose suddenly washed over him supplying Lucas everything he needed to continue the day as planned.

After hours of walking, exploring, and talking with strangers, Lucas felt worn and weary. The worst of it was he did not feel as though he made much progress beyond showing himself he can, in fact, do the uncommon and weird, yet be appreciated. He needed more.

As he continued walking aimlessly thinking about what he had observed, the evening approached giving him once again the inclination to head home, but something within urged him to walk just a few more streets before calling it quits. Lucas had grown to trust this feeling but still hesitated to act on it. Nonetheless, he kept walking. Many people passed him, though he paid them no attention. He was finished observing for the day.

To his annoyance, a homeless man stopped to ask him for something. Lucas couldn't hear the man's question over the passing traffic, but he waved the man away and said he did not have anything.

"I'm not asking you for money." The man said with a smirk on his face. "There's a McDonald's over there. Could you buy me some food?"

"No, I'd rather not," replied Lucas, and he walked past the disheartened man. Lucas did not think about the reasonable request, one he normally would agree to but was too deep in thought to be disturbed. His response was automatic originating from the social conditioning he received growing up: *Tell bums no!*

He crossed the street when a series of thoughts struck him. *Why did I treat the man that way?* he questioned. *How can I search to help myself, yet ignore the needs of others? Besides, there's something to be learned from him.* He turned around and walked back towards the man.

The man saw Lucas coming and seemed to understand the meaning of Lucas' eye contact. The man approached Lucas as Lucas approached him, though the man's face took on a sinister expression. Lucas was quite aware of the look, but thought nothing of it. After all, he did just treat the man poorly, and he felt he deserved it. The man was probably upset and was now suspicious of his motives, but Lucas felt at ease with the man, like he was in control.

"I'll buy you some food, if you tell me all you know about living on the streets." Lucas proposed.

The man's face turned to surprise as he asked "Why?"

"Because, there is something to be learned from you. I'm on a journey to understand this city and its people. All of its people. And, I think you can provide me valuable insight into homelessness and the homeless."

"Alright, but how about you give me fifteen dollars so I can stay at a bunk house tonight," requested the man.

"But, I don't have any cash," replied Lucas.

"There are ATMs around," the man pointed out.

"Okay, I'll give you the money."

"Great, I'll sit on that bench over there," he pointed to their left "and wait for you."

"Fine, I will be back shortly." With that, Lucas entered a building looking for an ATM. He checked to make sure the man was not following him, because in the event the man decided to rob him, he wanted to be alert. As he approached the ATM, Lucas gave one final look at his surroundings, but the man was nowhere to be found. Lucas withdrew a twenty dollar bill and headed back to their rendezvous. The man was still there.

"Let's go to the McDonald's anyway. I'm thirsty," said Lucas.

The man shrugged "Alright."

Lucas held on to the money afraid to give it to the man until they had their conversation. They walked together side by side as they talked.

"Tell me about your journey," said the man.

"I'm lost. Nothing is clear to me anymore. I remember a time when I believed in certainty, but that was a while ago." Lucas stared ahead in thought. "I need to find the meaning behind existence. The meaning for me at least. I'm tired of reading books and living in theory. I want to touch truth with my two hands."

"That's an interesting goal." The man seemed to have developed a respect for Lucas. "How will you do it?"

"That's the mystery and the adventure. At the moment, I'm stabbing in the dark hoping I will stumble onto the right path. I think I want to walk across the U.S. to observe society from an objective point of view. My gut urges me to start with this."

"But, why are you interested in the homeless?"

"The homeless are those who can't survive in the current society for whatever reason," explained Lucas. "By understanding why they have difficulty conforming to society, I hope to discover some flaw in the homeless, in society, or in both that causes their exclusion."

Passersby gawked as they watched a nicely dressed, young man walking with a middle aged, raggedy homeless man as though they were equals. Seeing this young man talking with such enthusiasm and passion to the homeless man as though a long history between the two existed baffled onlookers.

"Also," continued Lucas "I want to go directly to the source to get my information. I don't want to read about the homeless. I want to meet them and learn firsthand."

"Yeah, okay. I respect that."

"Another thing I'm interested in is how you survive on the streets. When I walk across the U.S., I plan to live in a tent, so I would really benefit from your knowledge."

"I just do whatever it takes to survive. Why do you want to travel that way?" asked the man.

"Well," replied Lucas "first and foremost, it's cheaper, which means I can start sooner. Though, the main point is to prove to myself that I can survive outside of society. You see, I feel like a slave to humanity and its creations which aren't built for me. I want to free myself."

"You'll never truly be free," the man warned. "No one is truly free."

"In a sense, you are right. If I'm not bound by my responsibilities to and reliance on humanity, I will be bound to the same of nature, but I find my only free choice is in the choosing of my master. Humanity is a part of the universe that has fancied itself supreme. I do not wish to enslave myself to such misguided beings. I wish to devote myself to the entirety of existence, not to a mere part."

"I think I understand. People have done that. Moved away from society to live with nature. You could do that as well."

"I've thought about it a little. This walk across the U.S. will help me decide if that's truly what I should do."

As Lucas and the man entered the McDonald's, Lucas offered to buy the man something, but the man insisted he did not want anything which took Lucas by surprise. Lucas, however, thought nothing further of it and ordered himself a drink. They sat together at a table.

For the first time since having met the man, Lucas started to notice the man's appearance in detail. Aside from the obvious raggedy clothes, ruffled hair, and black skin; Lucas noticed a strong yellow on the man's teeth, dirt streaked across his face, and a potent smell emanated from him.

"So, tell me your story however way you would like," said Lucas.

After a moment's pause the man began. "At an early age, I was put in a homeless shelter for youth, so when I turned eighteen, they kicked me out to end up on the streets. Eventually, I managed to get my trucker's license and got a job as a truck driver. I was able to buy a house, have a wife, and have kids. Then, things went backwards. My wife left me and took the kids. Later, I had a car accident while uninsured, so I lost my trucker's license and my job. I went back to the streets."

"Wow. To go so far to return to where you started. That's very unfortunate!" remarked Lucas angrily, then eagerly asked "So, what do you live for now? What purpose keeps you going?"

The man did not need to ponder the question but answered immediately. "Love. If I show people love, maybe I can impact someone's life. Maybe, I can help change the world. Just because I'm homeless doesn't mean I don't influence the world around me."

"Very true," agreed Lucas. "That's a noble purpose." Lucas, however, did not truly know what the man meant.

"Most see homeless people as something less than human, like animals. By showing people love and kindness, I hope to prove that we are just like them. Many homeless people aren't on the streets because they are crazy, lazy, or outcasts. Many are out there because life took a turn for the worse. Sure, there are those who are crazy, but that's only some of us. Life is hard, and people just don't understand how hard life can get. Sometimes, we lose our homes temporarily. That doesn't make us failures or worthless human beings. It means that times are tough for us at the moment, but things will improve.

"It bothers me when I see people walking past the homeless without any concern. They don't stop and ask, 'Hey, do you need some water?' They just walk past ignoring them. A man could be dying, and these people wouldn't stop to see if he needs help. People are saying, 'Don't feed the homeless.' What they are doing is leaving us to struggle or even worse, die. You'd think they would have compassion enough to help us get on our feet, but instead, they want to ignore us until we disappear. Well, we aren't going anywhere.

"This city creates homeless people. The only system really in place to help the homeless or those about to become homeless is welfare, but the government is trying to reduce or get rid of it completely. Without welfare, homelessness would rise." The man looked down at the table, then raised his head.

"And ironically, the city drops crazy people off on the streets and tries to hide it. People complain about the number of homeless people, but they don't realize the city *itself* is contributing to the problem. There's even a business based on the homeless. Shelters get our Social Security numbers to report to the government for funding, but they kick us out before we can even benefit from the funding.

"The way this city deals with the homeless has nothing to do with compassion. Those who help us have an agenda or something to gain. No one really helps us because we are humans in need of help. We are just another thing to exploit." A shudder ran through the man.

After a moment to digest, Lucas replied "I had no idea people have created a business off the homeless. That just sounds terrible."

"It is terrible. People have the power to help the homeless and prevent homelessness, but they choose not to." With this, the man let out a heavy sigh.

"This is very disconcerting. Surely, humanity could implement strategies that eradicate homelessness, like housing and food programs, and yet humanity chooses to allow it to plague not just this city nor this country but the world." Lucas, trembling from the gravity of this realization, grabbed his drink and took a sip. "Why? This doesn't make sense!"

A few of the other customers sitting nearby turned toward Lucas. Lucas caught the eye of a man twenty feet from him and quickly looked away. He decided he would have to watch how loud he spoke.

"Maybe, people are just that evil," continued Lucas. "People treat people badly in many ways. Homelessness is just one example. There's racism, sexism, and classism, but how can people be that evil? I try to think about my position. If I was born fifty years ago, would I be racist or sexist? I'm not now, but is that my nature or my circumstance? I wonder if those who are *evil* are so because it's their nature. I like to think these people merely act misguidedly, but I may just be naively optimistic."

"But, it does make sense. Well, kind of, and it's not necessarily because people are evil, even though many act like it, especially the ones trying to make a business off of us. But, programs already exist to assist those struggling to make ends meet or those with nothing at all. As early as the Revolution, this country has offered help to a small few, but we mostly expanded our programs after the Great Depression. Today, we have many, around at least a hundred government programs and countless foundations and charities, that attempt to provide support for as many people as possible, but these programs suffer from a massive lack of resources to truly accomplish their goals. Because of the limited funding, the people implementing these programs have to set criteria for who is most in need and who is deserving of help, and this is where the programs begin to undo themselves.

"What doesn't makes sense is how people decide who is most in need and who is deserving of assistance. When you begin to draw lines, your purpose falls apart because now you contradict the very reasoning you built your plans off of. To help. But with the limited funding, people are forced to act in such a way.

"I think this is planned. Not by the people trying to help, but the people regulating their efforts. See, power has always been associated with resources. The more you have, the more powerful you are, so I think those in power don't really want to help us. I think they give funding to people outraged by the living conditions of their fellow citizens only to appear to care and to help, but if they really cared and really wanted to help, there would be no limits to these programs.

Especially, the time limits on receiving help from welfare programs that Bill Clinton started. Yes, the idea that by shortening the timeframe people could receive assistance, people would feel compelled to remedy their situation sooner and are more likely to get back on their feet is a great idea if it were that simple, but it never has been and never will be."

"What do you mean?" interrupted Lucas. "Why are the constraints so ineffective?"

"Because, the problem has nothing to do with people forgetting about time or becoming complacent and needing motivation. The problem is much more complex. This limitation is just an easy way to force people into a direction without even dealing with the issues. It's the use of primal fears to goad people into action. An action many cannot even perform. A real solution must provide opportunities for growth and recovery from any and all afflictions psychological or physical, severe or minor. A real solution must penetrate to the core of a person and help him or her overcome the self-sabotage preventing progress and improvement. A real solution eliminates all obstacles external and internal and gives every person all the tools needed to construct their own lives."

"Yes, I absolutely agree!" exclaimed Lucas. "Why don't we do that?"

"Because, it takes a lot of work and a level of personal development people rarely achieve. At least, not enough to enact this. We await a new generation courageous enough to face their own imperfections and their developing selves, so they can grow and become the people capable of truly solving this problem and all other problems. We need gardeners or nurturers of humanity to save us from ourselves and help us grow, but we lack enough of these people. We lack these people because the majority of us choose not to see ourselves and face the challenges of growth. It's one hell of a cycle. Until we choose to break our cycle and grow, we can never become nurturers to help those unable to break the cycle."

"But it can be done! I know it can!"

"Of course, it can, but this is not a matter of capability but willingness and courage."

"I am not satisfied with this!" exclaimed Lucas. Then, remembering to control his volume spoke a little quieter. "Either humanity is misguided and unknowingly hurts itself, or it is us who are misguided in thinking something is wrong with humanity. This troubles me even more."

"Well, I believe in the bible. Nowhere does it say to treat your fellow man this way. It tells us to give and show love to all, and that means helping them grow and overcome all obstacles."

"I wish I had a faith so easily relied upon, however, I cannot accept anything not adequately reasoned out. If we take a step out of our morality and contemplate the possibility that right and wrong are more uncertain than we have been taught to believe, I find it impossible to make a moral judgment of the current structure of society. I think the only way to make any judgement is to assess the effectiveness of the current structure of society to emulate the values and fulfill the needs of those who live in it."

The man shuffled in his seat twisting and turning. He also adjusted his shirt and pants. Lucas stopped to watch the man.

"Oh! Don't mind me. I'm just getting comfortable. Keep going."

"Now, I don't have the knowledge necessary to achieve this assessment, but when I look at the people walking on the streets and driving in their cars, I see an overabundance of misery. Far too much misery for an effective societal structure. I watch people hurry to get to some place somewhere for some reason, but I hardly ever see people rushing to enjoy what's right in front of or inside them. They are always looking for something, but never finding it. Though I may be ignorant, I don't think this society emulates people's values nor fulfills their needs to be happy."

"You may have a good point," said the man. "I see many people every day while out asking for money. Some of them look more miserable than me, and I'm homeless!"

"I think the most important question is: who influences control over how society functions?" Lucas straightened himself as passion coursed through his body. "Those who influence the structure of society, its values, norms, morality, and its subjugation of people, must have some idea of how society should be. At least, to them. We need to find out just what that is. This will tell us what our society is emulating and hopefully, explain why society doesn't emulate the values of the people.

"I assume that the majority of the people do not have much influence over society given their discontent. If they had a great deal of influence, then would that which they take issue with be so prevalent?"

"You know, a lot of people have the same problems with the way things are, yet things don't change much," added the man. "I think it's obvious that a greater number of people oppose change."

"That makes sense since we live in an alleged democracy, but let's narrow our focus to one issue to better investigate. We have already established formally that 'all men are created equal,' however racial inequality still exist."

"True, this definitely is a Whiteman's world," said the man.

"But, if all men are equal, why do we continue to operate under the presumption that nonwhites are inferior?" After pausing to think, Lucas continued. "I see two possible explanations at the moment. Either the majority of people are racist, thus racial inequality continues despite attempts of the few to eradicate it, or the majority of people are not racist, but due to their lack of influence, they cannot counteract the racial inequality created by the few. I cannot think of any other explanation for the persistence of an idea we supposedly destroyed decades ago."

"I can't either," mumbled the man, "but there's always something."

"So, either racial inequality exist because the majority of the people of this country choose to keep it alive, and the government, being a democracy born amongst slavery and racial inequality, still has little power to override the influence of the majority, or it exists because an elite few designed society that way, and the people, in their current position, must acquiesce, thus contradicting the notion we live in a democracy. These possibilities should also explain why other social controversies such as gender inequality, same-sex marriage, LGBT rights, and homelessness still exist. Well, maybe they could explain any controversy."

"You know, I've never thought about it this way. Could there be a third possibility? Maybe, a third group influences both the people and the elite few."

"What do you mean?" asked Lucas

"Well, this third party would be separate from the government and the people, but it would have great influence over both. This group would influence and control society from the outside. I'm thinking of corporations, foreign governments, and any other big third party entities."

"That's an interesting thought."

"Also, this group may have had a part in the design of society if they were around for its formation and are trying to manipulate it today. Maybe, they are the one's keeping alive ideas that society has already destroyed and are reintroducing them to society." The man looked quite pleased with his statement.

"As you say this, I think of diseases that have essentially been eradicated from our country like polio, small pox, and the bubonic plague. Even though these diseases have been vaccinated against or contained, it is still possible to infect some people if we had live samples of the pathogens responsible for the diseases. If we think of all social inequalities as the diseases and the ideas behind inequalities as the pathogens, I think your point becomes easier to imagine."

"That's a good analogy! I have always wondered why inequalities still exist. Our constitution claims we are all equal, and further legislation reinforced this idea." Silence overtook them as both pondered the points raised. Then, the man continued "I just don't understand what there is to gain from keeping inequality alive."

Immediately, Lucas replied "power, security, and slave labor for starters."

"Maybe, but is all that necessary? Seems like a lot more trouble than it's worth."

"I say yes for the current structure of society, but perhaps, in another societal structure it wouldn't be. How exactly this other structure would look like, I'm not sure, but we can't possibly be limited to this one structure."

"I always wondered if there is a better way for things to be. I mean, why all this?" The man surveyed the McDonald's and what lay beyond the widows.

"I wonder the same, and I am surprised there aren't more people wondering the same thing. With all the misery I see, I assume people would be more inclined to ask if their lives have to be so miserable. Perhaps, we can develop a better design, and life could be better for all. I don't see a reason we can't or shouldn't try."

"The only thing stopping us from creating anything different is ourselves." The man looked to his left, then looked back to Lucas. "I hear people using excuses all the time saying 'we don't have enough resources, people are too stubborn, it's impossible to change everything,' or 'things will essentially be the same'. Worse than that, I think some people don't even realize things are bad."

"I think you're right. The only obstacle is our own awareness. People who use excuses like those must not be aware of the power they inherently have."

"Also, fear. Some are aware of the power they have to change things, but they are too afraid to use it. Going against the grain brings a lot of trouble to you. People want to feel safe and comfortable, so they don't challenge things."

"I guess we skipped another, though I find it hard to believe. Contentment. Perhaps, some are happy the way things are, but I don't think these people are as aware as they may think. We only do what we think is ultimately good, so in order for people to truly be content, they would have to perceive the way things are as ultimately good."

"I find that hard to believe too," concurred the man. "I can see people thinking it is better now than it ever has been. The only other option is that they find joy in the misery of others, but I don't think that's the answer."

"I hope not. This, however, poses another big issue. Again, we are faced with the invalidity of the perspective of either the people who think things are good or us, who think otherwise. If their perspective is invalid, then they must not be aware of it. If our perspective is invalid, then our sense of morality is very wrong, and we have been fed worthless notions all our lives. Both possibilities are troublesome."

A party of six walked past their table, and as they did so, one of them clumsily bumped into Lucas causing him to knock his drink on the floor. Surprise showed on Lucas' face, but the man looked amused.

"I'm so sorry!" gasped a rather beautiful girl about Lucas' age.

Lucas blushed. "It's quite alright."

"Let me buy you another drink."

"No, that's not necessary. The cup is still useable. I'll just refill it."

"At least let me help you clean up." she demanded.

Lucas and the girl went to grab napkins. Both came back with two handfuls each. Together, they dropped their napkins on the small puddle of soda and began to wipe up the spill.

Determined to continue his conversation, Lucas looked up at the man while kneeling on the floor and said "let us have faith in ourselves for the moment and follow the sentiment that our point is the valid one. This would mean that those who think things are good think this way because they remain unaware of the true nature of things. They may see what we see, but they would not entirely understand the ramifications of what they see. To them, inequalities would look good and necessary, or inconsequential."

"Or they don't see the inequalities at all. They could just be blind," added the man.

"I suppose we should consider that as well. At any rate, if this is the case, then their contentment is false, born out of misconception, not reality. Well, false in substance at the very least. Because their contentment is a hollow one, it can easily crumble under the weight of awareness. Once they become aware, they could never find contentment in the way things are ever again."

"That would mean we could overcome this obstacle by simply showing those people how bad things really are."

"Yes, you can show people, but they must choose to see. If they keep their eyes closed, it's pointless," interjected the girl. "I'm not sure you can convince people to become aware. They must convince themselves."

Lucas stopped his wiping to observe the girl. She wore tight jeans and a form fitting t-shirt, which he thought complemented her body quite well. Her hair was jet black and her eyes had a hue of stunning green. But, what captured his attention the most was her simple, yet sophisticated manner of carrying herself. When he looked at her, he did not see pretensions, nor a reactionary mode of thought. She seemed in tune with everything around her, responding to the essence of all things. "That's a very good point," he said. Then, he continued cleaning.

"That might make them the most difficult obstacle," commented the man, who seemed delighted to have another join the conversation.

The girl looked at the man and gave a knowing smile. "People are always your most difficult obstacle." As she spoke, she ceased cleaning up the spilt soda, but started again before looking down. Lucas, after finishing his half, moved on to help the girl finish hers as she continued the wiping motions that brought their hands into direct collision.

Lucas froze, unsure what to do but finding he had no desire to pull his hand away. His hand shook with nervousness. His eyes fixated on the floor.

The girl covered his hand with her own and firmly grasped it, rubbing the back of his hand with her thumb.

A warmth unlike anything Lucas had felt before soothed his tensing body and calmed his shaking hand. Slowly, he looked up from the floor to meet her vibrant green eyes gazing at and through him. *She's beautiful.*

Suddenly, she leaned forward and kissed Lucas on the lips, then pulled away.

"W-why?" Lucas struggled to speak through the shock and euphoria.

"Because, you're beautiful." She smiled the sweetest smile Lucas had ever seen directed towards him. After a moment, she returned to cleaning up the spill, and Lucas joined her.

When they finished, the girl addressed him once more. "I will see you again, and the next time we meet, I will give you my name,"

Lucas looked both perplexed and amazed. "What? How do you know?"

Again, she smiled that sweet, knowing smile. "My heart told me. But, now, I must go." She gathered all the soda drenched napkins, stood abruptly, and walked back to her group. As soon as she approached, her party enveloped her, one taking the bundle of napkins from her, and guided her out the door. She was gone.

"Goodbye." Lucas whispered after her.

Lucas turned back towards the homeless man as he rose from the floor. The man could not hide his grin and nodded his approval. Lucas nodded back, awe still showing on his face and continued. "Perhaps people are our greatest obstacle, but the foundation to their obstruction is awareness. Fear, for instance, comes from the notion of danger. Those who fear change do so because they believe change will harm them in some way. If, however, the change we suggest is only beneficial, then their fear becomes unwarranted with no rational justification. Those who would stop beneficial change out of fear can only do so because they remain unaware of its benefit. So, the ultimate obstacle is awareness, and all other obstacles are manifestations of this. The only obstacle is the greatest possible."

"That is if our point is valid." replied the man. "Well, it would be true for both sides. If we are right, then they must face awareness, but if we are misguided, then we must face awareness. Looks like awareness is the only obstacle for any of us."

"Very true, but that poses, perhaps the greatest issue of all." Lucas spoke slowly as if carefully painting an image with his words. "How do we achieve awareness? This question has underlined every point we put forth. We spoke of awareness as though humanity already possess it, as though awareness is something humanity is aware of, however, I doubt that.

"The position we find ourselves in urges us to discover the validity of our or the opposition's awareness before we can go any further. To do this, we must first discover awareness itself. My question is if we are unaware, how do we become aware? If we are unaware, then can we look within for awareness? If not, the alternative is to look without.

"Many times I thought I knew something only to find I did not. No difference appeared between the valid and the invalid ideas. If not for some outside influence indicating which is which, I could not tell the difference. If I cannot perceive the difference between the valid and the invalid without assistance, then how can I trust in my alleged awareness? Furthermore, is all of humanity in the same position as me? If so, how can I trust their awareness?"

"Man, those are some tough questions! You make it sound like we can't know anything."

"That's kind of what I'm saying, though I didn't realize it."

"You know, things could be a lot simpler if we solved this with the heart instead of the head."

Lucas looked confusedly at the man. "What do you mean?"

"We could feel the solution instead of thinking through all these complicated avenues of logic, and I think this is the only way. In fact, the heart has a way of navigating these issues much better than the head."

Lucas laughed. "Oh, how I wish I could leave it at that, but I wouldn't be me if I could. I regret to say that will never satisfy me. We have a gift of reason, and if I don't use it to the fullest, I fear it would result in a tragic waste."

"You may be trying to do the impossible," warned the man. "Logic does not touch all realms of our consciousness."

"That may be, but I have to try," retorted Lucas.

"I used to ask impossible questions, still do occasionally, but I find that trying to figure out how to live without the answers more beneficial." The man stood up abruptly. "Can we move to another place? I don't like being in one place for too long."

"Yeah, sure. Where do you want to go?" asked Lucas.

"We've been sitting for a while now. Can we walk around for a bit while we talk?"

Lucas nodded his assent, and the two exited the McDonald's together. The sun managed to sink beneath the horizon and an illuminated darkness engulfed the city without either's cognizance. Hardly anyone roamed about except for the business men just leaving work, teenagers full of angst looking for adventure, and the homeless who will spend the night on the streets. Fewer cars drove past. The unexpected change of scenery startled Lucas.

"When did it become dark?" asked Lucas. "It just snuck up on us."

"I guess we have been talking that long," responded the man. "Do you still want to keep talking?"

Lucas felt safe when the sun was up and people crowded the streets, but now, his confidence wavered. The man seemed trustworthy so far, however, Lucas could not help imagining the worst scenarios. For whatever good it served if any at all, Lucas asked the man "can I trust you?"

This time the man seized his opportunity to laugh. He laughed a deep, warm, and genuine laugh, which reassured Lucas a little. Once the man caught his breath, he said "there's only one way to find out. You have to see for yourself."

Lucas hesitated a moment, then replied "I suppose you are right. Perhaps, I should take counsel from the maxim 'nothing ventured, nothing gained'."

"The choice is yours. If you decide to stay, I'm available all night," said the man with a grin.

"Alright, let's keep talking," decided Lucas. "I have nowhere to be either, so I can see this conversation to the end."

"Great!" exclaimed the man. "I was worried we weren't going to finish. It has been a very long time since I've had such good conversation."

"Well, you lead the way."

The man paused, raised his hand and stuck his index finger in the air. He rotated until he found himself where he started. "We should go this way," the man said as he pointed to the left. "I feel the world pulling us in this direction. If we follow the current, hopefully, we will have better luck with our thoughts."

The man's strange behavior tempted Lucas to inquire, but he decided against it. "Alright," replied Lucas.

Lucas and the man rested their minds, meditating on their surroundings as they walked. Of course, they couldn't prevent their thoughts from returning to the conversation, but neither spoke. Lucas finally broke the silence.

"There's no point in living if we don't try to grow, to reach beyond ourselves and our time. Striving to do the impossible makes life worth living."

"Maybe," said the man. "Striving to achieve the unachievable may give life purpose, but it does not provide a means for living. We might have a direction to travel, but how do we survive the road?"

"I see your point, I think," replied Lucas. "It's like this intersection before us. We know we want to head straight across, but knowing that does not help us cross the street. We need to follow the crossing signal, look for oncoming cars, and walk at the appropriate speed."

"Yes, and we know to do this because a system was created," added the man.

"We rely on this system to cross the street, and if we didn't have a system, we would each make up our own before crossing. So, the direction we wish to travel and the means for traveling are separate entities," concluded Lucas.

The man nodded his agreement, then continued "Also, there are different ways to cross. We could play it safe and follow the system, or we could jaywalk, cross without looking, or cross very slowly. All of these could get us across, but some are safer than others."

"Okay," said Lucas "but what exactly are you saying?"

"We need to figure out which way of living is best for us as individuals and for humanity as a whole. Once we figure out how to live, we can really begin striving to do the impossible with confidence. We can live knowing things are right for us and that we will be healthy and happy. Living is separate from seeking an understanding of life, and we won't be able to understand life if we can't figure out how to live."

"Many people believe we have already found the right method, and are living by it, but I do not think so. As I was saying earlier, I see too much misery to think we found the best way to live, but how do we know what the best way to live is if we don't have a clear understanding of what we want life to be or how it should be?"

"Again, the direction and the road are two separate things. What we want life to be is the direction, and how we achieve our vision is the road. But, most important of all is how we live along the way. If we survive or thrive or die, all depends on us. We must choose to take care of ourselves, to ensure our health and sanity, and we don't need to understand life or what we want it to be to do so. We only need to listen to our bodies and our minds. They will guide us easily enough."

"I want to say we still need an understanding of life, however, when I consider children I think otherwise. Children learn how to survive well before they understand the workings of the universe. They learn how much food and drink they need to satisfy their cravings. They learn what keeps them warm and safe and to fear dangers. It seems they follow an instinctual guideline for everything. Once they develop sufficiently for survival, they, then, look at the bigger pictures, slowly understanding more and more. Looking at their example, I assume a similar method would work for us."

"We are alive. Could we really be lacking anything necessary for living?"

"Well, if our existence implies our knowledge of how to live then why aren't we living the best way now?" retorted Lucas.

"I've been asking myself that for years! Why aren't we? Maybe, it's because we have been taught to mistrust ourselves. Only after years of suffering, did I realize to listen to that little voice inside that shows what is right and wrong for me. The voice acts as a compass guiding me on my path, and wherever it points, I feel a force of will so great I can never escape it no matter how hard I try. I feel this will is beyond me. Not my own, but God's flowing through me. I think we all have this force within us, guiding us. I know that when I listen to this voice, I am happy and as much as it is in my control, healthy. When I don't listen, I am miserable and do things that jeopardize my health."

"The same force drove me to you today. I passed you with no intention of thinking twice of my decision, but suddenly a force overtook me. I had no choice but to talk to you. I agree, there is some sort of internal compass guiding our lives, however, I hesitate to give the credit to God. I tried avoiding this, but it, now, seems inevitable that I address this point.

"I do not believe in Christianity nor any other organized religion, rather I believe in my subjective experiences and reasonings, which together form my very own religion. A religion only for me. I will spare you the details, but what is most important of my beliefs is the necessity to establish an unshakeable foundation for all reasonings and beliefs. Thus, I must scrutinize further the origin of this force."

"Okay. Well, I will respect your beliefs. If this force doesn't come from God, then where?"

"Given that we each have this guiding force and all live different lives, some contradictory to others, I, first, want to consider this force to be not one but many. Assume each of us have a force characteristic to our individualities and that it does not come from anything but ourselves. This force would, then, be a part of us like our nature or disposition. If this is the case, then when we allow ourselves to follow its pull, we live only of and for ourselves. Our lives are born from the purpose within and ultimately seek the best way of living for our individualities. This way of life would not explicitly be best for the whole of humanity.

"If, however, we think of the force as one entity with different forms, following its pull would result in our fulfillment of some grand design created by God or simply characteristic of existence. This could only mean that our way of life would be best for humanity as a whole, though not explicitly best for the individual."

"The force exists. Does it matter where it comes from? If it comes from ourselves or from a grand design, won't the result be the same?"

"I suppose you are right. The only possible difference resides in our choice to allow this force to guide us. Discerning its origin only serves to help me decide whether or not to follow its pull, however, regardless of its origin, ignoring this force would equate to ignoring my sight and trying to live blind."

"That sounds very foolish. Maybe, what we see isn't real or complete, but it is all we have to see. Why should we disregard a sense so engrained in our lives?"

"I feel encouraged to abandon not just this internal force but all my senses because I believe in their fallibility. This must be the point you were making. I mistrust myself."

"Yes, our senses can fail us at times, but what are we left with if we abandon them?"

"Nothing, we are senseless."

"Then, why would you abandon the only thing guiding you?"

"Well, so reason can take control. I have been taught to prize reason above all. Reason is the most infallible, and it will be a better guide."

"Do you really believe that?" The man asked with a smile wide across his face.

"Yes, of course! Life is nothing more than a series of phenomenon that occur in some orderly fashion despite how chaotic they seem. Reason is the only tool we have to gain an understanding of these phenomenon."

"True, but is reason separate from the senses?"

"Perhaps… Reason is separate from the senses, yet it is built upon them. Without the information provided by the senses, reason would have no material in which to manifest itself."

"So, when you abandon your senses, do you also abandon reason?"

Lucas let out a sharp laugh. "That is what I implied isn't it? But, yes, it seems so."

"Well, what do you rely on for guidance then?"

"If I abandon reason, the only guidance left is the lessons taught by my parents, school, and the rest of society."

"Sounds like the only alternative is to let others tell you how to live."

"Indeed, this must be your point. By mistrusting ourselves and abandoning our senses, thus reason, we subject ourselves to a dependency on others for a method of living. Our lives, then, are not our own; they do not emulate our beings. Instead, our lives emulate the reasonings of others. On a grand scale, this could lead to an entire society living in dissonance and misery. This also suggests that the social inequalities we were discussing earlier and any other issues of similar origin could exist because the society fails to live by its own reasonings. That must be what the lack of awareness is: an abandonment of the senses and reason!"

"You only have part of it. I'd say there are three parts to awareness. The first is the guiding compass that compels us at our very core, our souls."

"Or our existence." Lucas added. "It shapes, no, it is the expression of our existence."

The man nodded and continued. "This is our ultimate guide and in my opinion, the most important of the three parts. The second is the head or the pure intellect. Our reason." Lucas nodded and gestured for the man to continue. "The head calculates possible ways to follow the compass and makes our path efficient. The third is the heart or the emotions that help us choose from the possible paths the head has calculated. When healthy and sound, the heart uses love, compassion, and courage to guide our decisions."

"So, the lack of awareness is the disruption of all three parts by abandoning or depriving the senses?"

"Yes, however, disrupting someone's guiding compass is not an easy task and cannot be done by simply depriving them of their senses. That will only affect their head and heart."

"Then how do people lose their guiding compass?"

"I don't think anyone can lose it. It is a part of you. As long as you live, you will feel its pull. You can only ignore it or be distracted from it."

"Distracted! That explains why we have so many distractions: TV, drugs, parties, movies, amusement parks…" Lucas trailed off as the list grew and grew in his head.

"That could very well be why." The man's tone implored caution.

Lucas returned from his tangent. "Well, I guess we can never know if we are ever truly aware, but we do have our senses which provide the foundation for our rational and emotional perceptions which in turn are guided by our compass. We have no choice but to stand by ourselves. Otherwise, we are cast into oblivion."

"Or, into the control of others."

"Exactly. We must embrace what awareness we have as individuals and trust in ourselves. I believe this to be the key to our ascension to higher planes of existence, to an elevation of our cultures and social paradigms."

"We figured it out then?"

"Well, I don't know. We did not identify awareness with any certainty at all. At least, it still seems too ambiguous without definite shape to me. I don't think we accomplished much at all."

"One thing, we decided to trust ourselves. That's an accomplishment. I'm certain you will understand and feel the relationship of the three parts as you experience more."

"Perhaps, but what if we make a mistake? What happens when our fallibility inevitably shows itself?"

"So, we stumble. Maybe, even fall. Can't we get back up and keep moving forward?"

"I suppose we could try, but again we merely act on a faith in ourselves. It seems all we can accomplish in this matter is a faith in ourselves."

"Or a faith in God."

"Or existence, but a faith nonetheless. I wanted something certain, something based in reason, but I don't think I am capable of such a task."

"That's because you aren't. Existence is beyond human reasoning. Look, we already said that we couldn't gain an understanding of life unless we figured out how to live. It's the same here. We need to follow our guiding compass with our head and our heart even if we cannot reason why. When we figure out how best to live, then we will be able to strive for understanding."

"Yes, you're right, but I didn't realize how daunting our situation is. Now, I feel the weight of it all. In order to understand existence, we need to increase the capacity of our reason. I don't know if that's even possible. I'm afraid to go on."

"I don't think we have a choice. At this point, we have gone too far to turn back."

"Not only that. I think my life has been on the verge of this transition. Just the other day, I did some brain storming to figure out where my life is going and what I need to do. After sifting through nonsense, one phrase revealed itself and refuses to leave. I cannot stop thinking 'rise from the mud,' though I'm not completely sure what it means. I have a feeling it has something to do with what we are discussing and more. Some sort of overarching cognitive theme."

"That sounds interesting. What do you mean by mud?"

"When I think of mud, I think of a thick, slimy, sticky substance that hinders movement. I think the metaphor symbolizes those ideas and thought processes that hinder higher thinking. Those ideas that prevent growth and encourage complacency. Also, it's the starting point of our sentience."

"Starting point?"

"Yes, like the theories of the primordial slime or primordial soup."

"I'm not sure I know what those are."

"They theorize the origins of life, though perhaps, not accurately. Their common theme is a place where life formed randomly by chance. Furthermore, life could only exist in simple forms until the environment, by chance, became suitable for more complex life forms. Similarly, I imagine such an origin for our sentience. By chance, our sentience came to be, and by chance epiphanies or chance encounters, our sentience grows. It seems a randomness is inherent of our existence, but this does not suffice for me. I don't want to rely solely on chance to rise to higher planes of thought. I want to climb out of the mud and seize a broader horizon. I don't see why I or anyone shouldn't strive for this."

"But before you can rise from the mud you must first learn to live in it."

"That's what it seems like, but I don't want to have to live in the mud! I just want to break free. Is it absolutely necessary?"

"Whether it's necessary or not, you are in it. You have no choice but to learn to live in it, unless you know how to get out."

"I don't know. That's the problem. I don't know!" Lucas turned away from the homeless man in an attempt to hide the tears beginning to seep from his eyes. He gave up hiding and turned back. "I can't stand being so ignorant, so naïve, so incapable! How many wrongs have I committed? Too many! I just want to know what is right. I just want everything figured out, so I can stop making mistakes. I am incompetent. I can't..." Lucas sat down on the curb, and with his head in his hands, he wept between his knees.

The man reached out to touch Lucas on the shoulder, but pulled away just before making contact. He stepped towards Lucas, then, turned away. Awkwardly wobbling to the building adjacent to them, the man approached the wall placing his hands above his head and using them for support. He threw his head back and gazed longingly at the night sky. After a few moments, the man walked over to Lucas and sat beside him.

"You can't be so hard on yourself. You are expecting the impossible of yourself."

Between gasps of air, Lucas croaked "I know, but I must try. If I don't, who will? Besides, I know I can't truly understand anything, but how am I supposed to keep living this way? What's the point of all this -- the buildings, the streets, the city, all of civilization, of existence -- if we are incapable of understanding any of it? Why am I sentient if I am condemned to ignorance?"

The man tried to answer but only managed inaudible mouthings of nonsense syllables. Both sat perplexed. Lucas, squinting in the hope that this would refine his thoughts, stared at a bird on the opposite side of the streets. The man leaned on his hands behind his back and returned to gazing at the sky. Both were closer than ever before, yet infinitely further away. Like mountains oceans apart, the two coexisted on a similar plane. Their altitude alone bound them together.

The first car in a long while drove past slowly with hip-hop music blaring. Across the street, a group of teenagers swaggered and laughed along the sidewalk oblivious to all but the witty remarks they exchanged with one another. A dog pranced by, ribs showing from malnutrition. Although Lucas and the man remained frozen in thought, the world carried on around them.

"How do I continue, when I know my efforts are futile?" asked Lucas.

"Just because you don't understand how you fit into the world doesn't mean you don't. You must be patient. If you are supposed to understand, you will, but only when the time comes. Meanwhile, take a look around. Don't you see the beauty of this place? Yes, there are ugly things here as well, but that can't diminish the beauty that already exists. Focus on the beauty, its presence, how it exists. Then, look at the ugly. What causes this ugliness, and how can you make it beautiful?"

"You make us sound like artists."

"We are. We created this civilization, and it reflects our vision of beauty. We create our lives as well, and they, too, reflect our vision of beauty. We have complete control over how we live within this world. We make this human world the way it is. But, we are imperfect, and our vision is sometimes blurred. Therefore, we must work to improve our creation by improving our vision. We may not understand this world nor the beauty of it, but we can be attracted to that beauty and nurture it."

Lucas, still wiping tears away, stood abruptly. "I have to go."

"Are you sure?" The man asked with a furrowed brow. "We can still talk it through."

"No, talking won't help me now. I have done all the thinking and talking I can. I need to go. I want to be alone."

"Okay, then. I hope you find what you are looking for. The road ahead may be difficult, but you must push on. If you give up, you will be miserable. You won't ever be happy until you solve this enigma for yourself. I will never forget this night or you. You've woken me from a sleep I was unaware of. I hope to see you somewhere great someday."

Agony continued to reverberate through Lucas as he struggled to remain present. All he could manage was a simple "Thank you. Good bye."

"Good bye," replied the man with a hint of sorrow in his voice. The man took one last look at Lucas. He thought of the first impression he had: an affluent, white male, young and unaware, unable to see beyond his own experience and contemplate the plight of others. Now, he laughed to himself though it did not show. Lucas had grown on him, taken him by surprise.

Before him was not a boy oblivious to all things outside himself, whose selfish desires led by the nose, rather the man saw a boy filled with purity and earnest curiosity. In fact, despite Lucas' youth, the man perceived a leader, someone well beyond himself. He had grown to revere Lucas. Had Lucas been a king and the homeless man a knight, the man would have sworn his life and loyalty to Lucas. He would accompany Lucas on his quest if only asked.

Lucas approached the man and with a trembling hand, shook his hand. Within their grasps laid the twenty dollar bill extracted from the ATM earlier that day. Both remained, hands clasped, for a long moment as they took what they thought to be their last look of one another. Lucas, finally, gave a solemn, silent nod, and the man reciprocated. He retracted his hand, turned, and walked opposite of their position.

Lucas could not think but one thought: *Home. I must get home.* A fog settled over his mind. All fluidity turned solid. All synaptic firing seemed to cease. The world became an imperceptible blur as he staggered and stumbled in a direction he hoped would lead him back to his car and then home.

The homeless man could not bring himself to move. Instead, he stood, watching Lucas travel as a blind person gropes through the world. Beyond Lucas, the horizon began to glow as the orb of life breached the gray of predawn. Slowly, rays of warmth touched the man's face, and a swell of hope burst within him. He felt that if his purpose had gone unfulfilled, he could now rest assured, for this night, if none other, achieved such a goal. The man knew Lucas would become something great one day. Perhaps, a seer of truth, a prophet, or simply a man pure of heart. Whatever would become of Lucas, the homeless man was grateful to play a role, however small, within his journey.

THE MEETING

The car ride passed Lucas without notice. Next thing he knew, he had already parked and climbed out of his car somewhere downtown. He began walking in what seemed to him a random direction, but his guiding compass insisted it was towards purpose. The evening was approaching, the sun setting on the horizon casting shadows in Lucas' direction as the last of its rays caressed his face. He watched as the sun slowly sank beneath the horizon.

People bustled about exploring the nightlife for pleasurable experiences to distract them from the daily toil and moil. Lucas looked past, no, through these people as if they were translucent apparitions. He was here to meet someone, someone who would appear whole in a hollow world.

Many people passed him, though none stood out. Lucas could not tell any difference between a whole or hollow person, but his guiding compass led him through the mass of people. As he approached one person, a force would repel him in the opposite direction causing him to weave through the crowd in an unusual pattern. He continued in this manner until he reached a particular intersection.

The world flowed around Lucas as he stood watching a young man cross the street. This young man towered over Lucas at a height of six feet. He wore his long, wavy, black hair in a ponytail held back with a black bandana. Donned on his feet were a pair of gray suede wingtip oxfords. Dark grey dress pants hung from his waist, and a shirt with a printed rib cage covered his torso. On his back rested a bag adorned with blankets and a pillow rolled into a tight cylinder and harnessed to his bag with rope. Out of an opening of the main compartment, a wooden baseball bat protruded just within arm's reach, so that if the situation required, the young man could wield it easily enough. But, what stood out the most to Lucas was the swagger so prominent in the strides of the young man's steps. The alluring air of confidence resonated with Lucas. *This must be the one I am to meet.*

The young man glided past Lucas not appearing to recognize the awe and determination with which Lucas stared at him. Lucas wavered for a moment in his trust of the compass and questioned the validity of this new direction. After the young man put half a block between them, Lucas gasped at his hesitation and hurried towards the young man at a slow jog, ceasing when a fast walk would finish the job.

"Hey! Excuse me," Lucas breathed between deep inhalations. The young man did not hear or pay attention, so Lucas cried out once more. "Excuse me, guy with the bat!"

This time the young man turned around to find Lucas at his heels. Surprised but receptive, the young man asked "Yeah, what's up?"

"I'm sorry to bother you, but the universe has directed me to you. We are supposed to exchange what we have gathered from existence. I'm not sure what we are to learn, but I'm certain it will be a pivotal exchange."

The young man smiled. "I knew someone would approach me when I arrived in this city a month ago! My name is Alexander." He reached out his hand.

Lucas took Alexander's hand and replied "My name is Lucas. So, what's your story?"

"Let's sit down, and I'll tell you. I've been walking too long with my nerve damage and need a rest."

Alexander slid off his backpack and sat on the sidewalk with his back against a building. Lucas sat beside him and readied himself for the regaling of Alexander's tale.

"I'm from a small country town in Texas where I lived with my mom, my brother, and my sister. I left about a year ago to escape drugs and the people that followed them. My mom basically said 'I'm doing drugs. If you don't like it, leave.' So, I did, and it was the best decision I ever made. I really don't regret taking off with only the clothes on my back. I've had some pretty good fortune along the way. I managed to get all that I have now and some homes to stay at, but I prefer living on the streets.

"I first traveled to San Antonio, stayed a few months. Then I hitchhiked all the way to New Orleans, stayed there for a bit, and then felt it was time to come back to Texas. I got a lucky break long the way and found a truck driver willing to take me all the way to San Antonio. I thought we were close, so I told the guy to let me off. He seemed hung up about it for some reason, but he let me go. Turns out I'm on the other side of the state! That's how I ended up here, but it's all a part of the journey, man."

"Wow, that's a long way to travel by foot and hitchhiking. How safe was it?"

"I made it unharmed, but it's always a risk. A lot of shady people out there. That's why I have my bat." A proud smile ran across Alexander's face. "You always need to keep some form of protection with you."

Lucas' eyes moved to the bat, then to Alexander's backpack. "What all do you have in your bag?"

"Let me show you."

Alexander grabbed his luggage and began untying the ropes holding his cylindrical bundle of bedding. "I have two blankets, a sheet, and a pillow here." Once he untied the rope, he placed the bundle aside. Next, he pulled out the wooden bat. "I found this beauty in an abandoned house. This is probably my favorite."

Lucas accepted the bat and felt its weight. A well balanced bat that glided easily through the air with the rotation of his wrist and fluid motion of his arm. His hand enjoyed the smooth, grainy texture of the wood. He took a couple swings then handed it back to Alexander. "I like the small size and that dark brown stain. It's more like a club than a baseball bat."

"Yeah, isn't it awesome?" Alexander put the bat with the bedding and began rummaging through the rest of his bag, placing each item in front of Lucas as he called them out. "I have spare rope, a notepad for songs and poetry, a can opener, spare clothes, an extra pair of shoes, toiletries, a special die and minor first aid stuff. Everything I need right here. Oh, and I have this water jug that has Powerade in it at the moment."

"Everything you need? That's not much. I find it hard to believe."

"Yeah, you would be amazed at how little you need to survive. You have all these things in your home, but most of it you don't need."

Lucas furrowed his brow incredulously. "I'll take your word for it."

Alexander began recollecting his belongings and returning them to the bag. As he grabbed his notepad, Lucas stopped him. "Can I read what you wrote?"

"Sure, it's a song, but you can read it as poetry."

As Alexander continued putting away his things Lucas read the lyrics slowly and intently trying to use his complete cognitive capability to comprehend it. Because he was here to learn from Alexander as well as give him all he could muster, Lucas wanted to absorb everything he could.

The song was written on a yellow note pad bent and crumpled by the cramped backpack and the constant travel. The hand writing, barely legible, remind Lucas of his own as he read and reread the lyrics. One line kept catching his attention: "Is it a suit and tie that divines me an animal?" In his hands, Lucas beheld the consequences of the social hierarchy. Here lay proof that Alexander had been cast to the bottom and of his failed attempt to understand exactly why and how he arrived there.

"I like this a lot. This depicts precisely what I am trying to understand, the consequences of the arbitrary divide of human worth. In this, you voice your confusion. Why won't people help you? Why can't you live the life you want?"

"Yeah man, I'm clueless. I don't understand why people can't just take care of each other."

"They judge your worth by your ability to adhere to the current paradigm. If you do not have a job, for example, or some other proof of productivity, then you are a waste of life, a worthless person."

"What the hell is a job anyways? There are no jobs in Mother Nature. I just want to live with Mother Nature. People lost the point. Life isn't about working. It's about realizing the beauty of the universe and trying to express that beauty."

Lucas smiled. "That was well said. I recently found that to be the only thing worth living for, expressing beauty and finding the beauty in everything, even what seems ugly. I knew I was meant to talk to you!"

"Yeah man, I'm feeling it too."

Lucas tensed as he struggled to ask "Do you mind if I hang out with you for a bit?"

"No, I don't mind!" Alexander grinned. "You can see what a day in the life of Alexander is like."

"Great, thanks!" Lucas said relieved.

Alexander stood and threw on his backpack. Lucas rose taking Alexander's lead. Then, both began walking towards the unknown, towards a world beneath the shadows, though neither knew the magnitude of their journey. Alexander swaggered coolly and with an ease disproportionate to the effort soon to be required of him, while Lucas focused on each step as though they were his last.

"I'll show you my home." The words flowed nonchalantly from Alexander as if he were oblivious to the paradoxical statement just uttered.

"You have a home? I thought you lived on the streets!"

Alexander chuckled "Yeah." He paused a moment savoring the confusion. "My home is under a bridge up on a shelf. You'll understand what I mean when I show you."

Lucas admired the humorous disposition Alexander managed to maintain despite his circumstances. Lucas pondered whether it is the personality of the individual or the circumstances themselves that produce such a serene state of being. Does the personality of one so tranquil inherently have less entitlement and expectations, or would anyone stripped of all control over oneself develop a forced acceptance of things? Is this humor a sign of strength or a loss of will?

"So what's your life project? Why do you exist?"

"Well, right now, my goal is to get my ID, so I can get a job and eventually an apartment. I like the streets and want to stay, but my sister was picked up by CPS. I have to help her out and give her a home with her family. My mom's in jail, and my brother is homeless too, so it's up to me. I want to help my mom and brother out as well, but my sister is my main focus since she's the youngest and can't really do anything about her position."

"Wow, that's great of you to do! Are you going to stay here or go back to where your sister is?"

"I think I'll go where she is. It'll be easier on her that way."

Lucas nodded and paused to think. "So, is that all you have planned? What about what you want to do for yourself?"

"Oh, yeah man! I've got plans." Alexander's face brightened, and he stood a little straighter. "I'm an artist, so I want to develop my art while traveling and sharing my art with the world. I'm thinking about being a welder to fund my travels. I have this dream of buying a boat and sailing the world, spreading love and beauty everywhere I go."

As Alexander spoke, each step seemed to carry them further into a world of their own, a realm of existence juxtaposed with the collective human universe like a bubble within a bubble, but which was within which was indeterminable as the boundaries of each alternated with every glance. Lucas felt a strange sensation of submersion and a subsequent dismantling of the scaffoldings of thought that held his mind in a particular shape. Now, his mind began to float and fold and unfold itself. Something was happening here, but he could not discern what.

"That sounds amazing! The freedom of thought required to construct such a notion as well as maintain it is enormous. The confines of your mind must be vast."

"Thanks, man! No one has really appreciated that before, at least not like that. In this city especially! The majority of people here give off so much negative vibes. Being here is pretty discouraging at times."

"I definitely understand what you mean. I find it extremely difficult to commit to yourself in a place that makes you feel so empty. It feels as if simply being authentically you cost you everything. Sure, there are those who appreciate you no matter where you are, but these are few and must be burdened with a similar plight."

Alexander reached into his pocket for a cigarette, brushed the hair out of his face, and then lit it. Each motion executed with a smoothness born from the ease of caring not for the world around. In that moment, only he and his cigarette existed. All other persons and things deemed inconsequential, but still this distraction remained relentlessly seizing his attention. He thought he might address it again.

"Do you want a cigarette?"

"No, I don't smoke," Lucas waved away the offer, "but thanks."

Alexander shrugged and took another hit of his cigarette. "So, what about you? What's your story?"

"Well, I have two ways I can tell you, the literal way or the metaphoric and abstract way."

"The abstract way seems cool."

"Alright then. I was born into a society deep within the mud of this universe. My people do not know how to be human, do not know how to act, think, or live. How they have survived appeared a mystery at first, but now, I realize we are supported by those slightly less deep so that we can do their bidding. We depend on those above us for everything. We are like children, infants, but productive infants. But, I was different from the rest. Always asking questions and absorbing everything, I hungered for more than what was offered, and I sought it out.

"I began to venture beyond the border of our village into the greater society surrounding ours. I ventured slowly, going a little further every time but afraid to go too far. On returning from my journeys, I would share what I learned, and at first, I was met with appreciation and encouragement. There came a time, however, when I venture further than any of my people before me, and this is when my sharing began to be met with resistance and rebuke.

"I didn't understand why they lashed out at me. I hadn't changed my behavior, and I could not yet comprehend the negative consequences of presenting such novelties to my people. The only option left to me at that stage of development was to internalize these incidents, and so I did. I began blaming myself, my method of presentation, my choice of content, my words, anything and everything I could imagine of myself to place blame. Eventually, I convinced myself I was crazy. My self-esteem became nonexistent. I had torn myself down ultimately, and totally. I had actively sought to destroy every parcel of my being. I tried to eradicate my psyche. It was as if my immune system designated my mind an invader and moved to eliminate it. I had rejected myself.

"There is no greater adversary than oneself and no greater plight than war with oneself. I guarantee that! And, I was to live in such a manner for the next fourteen years, though I never fully escaped. Despite this internalization and internal war, however, I, somehow, managed to observe and learn a great many things. I kept venturing out to find proof of my insanity.

"I think what enabled me to continue learning was when I finally positioned myself on the fence between the two contradictory possibilities, though I did lean towards insanity, or more accurately, I pulled myself towards insanity using the rope of false certainty attached to my people. I chose to accept my people's views as absolute, and thus I surrendered my psyche. The psyche, fortunately, is not so easily defeated.

"The deeper realms of my psyche, the ones I am not conscious of, resisted and fought back. The weapon of choice: doubt, infinite doubt. Keeping me in confusion stalled my complete surrender, buying my deeper consciousness enough time to gain more influential ground. And so, I began to dance along the fence. Swaying to one side, then, to another in an endless cycle. Each step met by another. Each pull matched by another. The dancing of wills. A mind split in two; each half trying to overtake the other. And, the stakes were high! To one edge an abyss of nothingness, a blackness so encompassing, I found it impossible to fathom what lay within, save for more and thicker mud. To the other, a mountain piercing the sky and beyond, a mountain of unbounded growth and understanding rising from the mud of my psyche. Which side I would fall remained unclear, but I was inevitably to fall.

"I speak as though I have already experienced an outcome, but the truth is I still dance on that fence. The dance, however, has changed.

"I danced relentlessly, because there was nothing else for me to do. I watched and absorbed as much as possible for evidence supporting either side. I tried to remain unbiased. Although I was split, the two halves pulled with equal force allowing no net bias, and the stalemate bided me time to gather more information. Slowly, over many years, I gathered enough evidence to destroy the notion of certainty that I should cast myself into the abyss. Unfortunately perhaps, I have yet to collect the necessary evidence to substantially give form to the claim of my deeper consciousness that an equally powerful certainty demands I leap to the mountain.

"And so, I dance and will continue to dance for however many eternities required. That's why I am here today, to waltz in pursuit of the mountain, and in you, I see a way, though it's not yet clear to me. I must rise from the mud!" Lucas looked at the ground in silence.

"Wow, man! I get that. Sounds pretty scary in a lonely kind of way. Being on your own without help or guidance and being your own worst enemy. Yeah, I totally understand."

They reached a construction zone and moved toward the base of some scaffolding. Alexander dropped his backpack and climbed onto a metal bar. Lucas followed suit, and both sat staring at the cluttered road in front of them. Debris, piled earlier that day, lay beside a shipping container sheltering various construction tools. Orange cones barred their side of the road from oncoming traffic. Dust and small scraps rustled and floated in the cool breeze. A rumbling noise permeated the air as cars drove past. All was the normal hubbub of the city.

Then, Alexander lifted his head and let out a loud, echoing howl. Confusion masked Lucas' face. Alexander repeated himself as if demanding a reply from the city. After a few moments of hesitation, Lucas let out a howl of his own, though quieter and more subtle.

"I don't understand why the homeless are considered so bad." Lucas sighed. "They're people are they not?"

"Yeah, but we're the outcasts, the lowest of the lows. A lot of people give the homeless a bad vibe with all the drugs they do and not trying to better themselves."

"But is that really your fault, or are you a product of the flaws in civilization? I like to think this is the case. If we acquire a true understanding of how and why the homeless exist, I guarantee we will find the fatal flaws of our civilization. Yet, it seems we consciously overlook them."

"That is intelligent, a very intelligent thing to say! I've never heard anyone say that before."

A warmth swelled in Lucas, and he could not help ginning. "Thanks" he said as he repositioned himself in an awkward fidget.

"I'll show you a street where a bunch of homeless people gather to sleep, after I show you my home, of course."

"Sure, that would be great! Then, I'll get a better idea of what's out here." Lucas hopped off the bar and landed in a squat. He rose and said boldly "let's go!"

Alexander smiled amused by the displayed enthusiasm for the opportunity to see his home and other homeless people. He still could not quite believe this encounter was real. It seemed so out of place that it must have been a dream. "Alright, let's go." Alexander jumped off and equipped his backpack.

Again, they strode deeper into the darkness of night, to the unknown, the unfathomable. As they walked, passersby gave little attention to the two, though some glanced conspicuously in their direction with undiscernible expressions of either confusion, disgust, or some other extreme. The two, however, did not concern themselves with such trivialities, for destiny approached, reaching from the horizon, pulling them with increasing force.

On their left, loud music blared from giant speakers in a bar only sparsely populated. The few inside divided themselves into categories. In one corner, people wearing gaiety on their faces gathered to bathe in each other's luminescence, however, dissatisfaction grew as each absorbed the energies of the others. Disappointment appeared to overcome them all, but they just intensified their efforts.

Another group huddled around a table with heads down as they peered into their glasses. One man looked up as if to say something, decided against it, and returned his watchful eye to his glass.

At the bar sat two pompous creatures of abhorrent bodily proportions. The two spoke at one another as if the other were merely a mirror and soundboard. The discourse consisted of two very distinct discussions, each being projected and received by the same individual. The creatures lifted their glasses in a toast and chugged the contents with a single gulp.

The bar slipped out of sight, and Lucas returned his attention to Alexander. "How much farther to your home?"

"It's just around the corner here. See that bridge? That's it."

Lucas hesitated at the crosswalk as he noticed the red-orange hand commanding him not to cross, but Alexander paid no heed and began crossing. Lucas, suddenly overcome with the urge to follow, threw his hesitations aside and stepped quickly in pursuit. Directly ahead, a parking lot gave lodging to the vehicles whose owners explored the nearby bars, restaurants and college. The parking lot started almost parallel to the road which became the bridge, then sloped down until it met the edge of a small park and maneuvered around to form an L-shape. Both lot and park continued to slope down to meet a large bayou.

Alexander weaved through the cars in a serpentine path, quite unnecessary yet brought him a sense of rawness, of thought uncorrupted by the influence of others' logic. Lucas remained in toe but chose a more linear route not quite able to suppress his logical compulsions preventing him from following Alexander's exact course. A soft crunch sounded as they reached the grass covering the extremity of the park.

"It's right over there." Alexander pointed to the under belly of the bridge. "We have to hop this fence to get to it."

Alexander quickened his pace and jumped grasping the top of the fence. His backpack swayed, but he managed to maintain his balance. He hurled himself over and signaled for Lucas to follow.

Lucas, stopping abruptly, asked "Is this illegal?"

"Probably, I think it's trespassing, but we should be fine. I've been staying here for about a month now."

Although Lucas hesitated only a second longer before proceeding, an eternity passed before him as he grappled with his hold on reality. The schematic tower on which he stood began to crumble. Never had he dared to defy human constructs so directly and at such an extreme since he pledged his loyalty to the fetters of adulthood. At this moment, Lucas did not feel as though he stepped forward, rather he felt to have traveled back through time to an earlier stage in his cognitive development, to a more basic perception. Now, he was redrawing and reconstructing his schematic tower.

The act of trespassing alone, Lucas knew, could not elicit such a sensation within him. He thought it must be something more. Perhaps, a cascading effect that began with his initial encounter with Alexander and slowly built up to this seemingly explosive moment without his noticing. Yes, he began this defiance by approaching this odd peer of his. How he managed to miss the building turmoil eluded him, but he realized the insignificance of the matter. Reality, or his perception of reality, was now breaking apart to take on a new form. All that mattered now was that he remain calm to maintain his sanity. Soon enough, his perception would take shape again, and so it did.

Relieved that clarity returned to him, Lucas grabbed the fence and threw himself over. As he landed, he felt an intensification of gravity's pull. This moment marked the birth of something.

Alexander led the way down a concrete walkway around construction equipment and finally, to a small hill of sand in front of the next fence to climb. Above, the underbelly of the bridge exposed itself, and past the fence, directly ahead, was one supporting base of the bridge marked by a slopping wall that reached twenty feet above ground.

"My home is up there." Alexander said as he pointed to the top of the sloping wall.

After climbing over the second fence, Lucas asked "And, how do we get up there?"

"We run up. See those things that look like steps? We run up over there and grab on to the first step. Then, we pull ourselves up to the next, and after that, we jump to the step to the left. Then we climb up to the top. It's easy. I'll show you."

Alexander ran up the wall, grabbed the first step, and hurled himself up. His backpack added a lot of extra weight, but he knew he could manage. He climbed up to the next step, and then removed his backpack and threw it to the top.

Lucas cringed as he watched Alexander make that final jump, which he estimated to measure six feet across. A three foot jump slightly to the right. Then, a one foot bounce to the left placing him back on the proper trajectory and propelling him the last two feet.

Then, he relaxed as Alexander climbed to the top about another six and a half feet up.

"Are you sure that's the only way up?" Lucas asked, fear showing on his face. "I don't know if I can do that."

"That's the way I do it, but I have some rope. I can pull you up."

A sudden awareness of the cowardice taking over him urged Lucas to accept the challenge. "No, I'll give it a shot." Lucas ran up the wall and pulled himself onto the first step. Next, he climbed to the second step about five feet above him. He looked at the final protrusion and moved to jump. At the last moment, he froze. The fear controlled him now. He rocked backward and forward imagining himself soaring through the air over a twenty foot drop.

"You alright?" Alexander asked.

"Yeah, just give me a minute."

Lucas studied the structure he climbed. He saw one other possibility, though it would require a great deal of upper body strength. The alternative necessitated he jump about a foot with arms raised directly above him. After he grabbed hold of the ledge above, he would need to slide to the left about eight feet, then pull himself up the to the top, all the while, hanging twenty feet above ground with nothing but the slopping wall to guide his fall to the concrete below.

He jumped up and barely took hold of the ledge above. Once he secured his grip, he began sliding to the left. Lucas felt the security of the step below disappear and the emptiness that took its place. The next part was the true test. In one jerky motion, Lucas brought his shoulders over the ledge and with another motion he lifted the rest of him over and rolled away from the edge. He lay there for a moment allowing himself to recover, then sat up to address Alexander.

"I did it!"

"Yeah, man. I've never seen anyone do it like that before, so props to you!"

Lucas smiled at the compliment and because of the elation he felt for thwarting a challenge. "So, this is your home."

Lucas stood and looked around. A flat area extended from the edge to the base of another slopping wall that led to another flat area providing only enough space to walk hunched over, which met the underbelly of the bridge. Equidistant columns rose from the edge to support the bridge, and five more rows ascended the other wall. To one side, a view of the bayou glistening in the moonlight. To the other, the park and the parking lot. Reflected moonlight danced on the columns and underbelly in beautiful waves flowing in all directions.

Alexander moved to sit on the other sloping wall and signaled for Lucas to join.

"This place is actually really cool." Lucas said as he took his seat beside Alexander. "You have a nice view and this beautiful display of moonlight. It's a beautiful place."

"I'm glad you can appreciate it. That's why I stay here. It has good vibes."

Alexander leaned over, pulled out a couple of cigarettes and rolling paper. He snapped off the filters and tore open the cigarettes spilling the tobacco into the cupped rolling paper. After the tobacco was in place, he rolled the paper. Lucas watched a little confused by the act but accepting it nonetheless. Then, he returned his attention to the dancing lights above him.

"You're something special." Alexander said as he moved to seal the paper with his tongue.

Lucas looked over at Alexander, saw him licking the edge of the paper and sealing the rolled cigarette with his complete attention on the task before him.

Alexander repeated himself, this time with his attention on Lucas. Lucas shot Alexander a puzzled look, then asked "Are you talking to me or the cigarette?"

With a laugh, Alexander said "I'm talking to you bro!" After settling down, Alexander continued. "Not many people still have that spark of life in their eyes and that intense and genuine curiosity the way you do. Whenever you ask something, I can tell you really want to know. You also think beyond what is generally thought. You're something special; there's no doubt about it."

Lucas held a roaring alarm in his head in check. Like all other compliments on his character or being he kept the incoming information at bay in the periphery of his consciousness. He could not let such words touch his core until he assessed their threat if any existed. Too many times had crippling jabs to his essence come guised in compliments. He need to inspect this statement, turn it over, and deconstruct it before allowing himself to disable his protective barriers and grant passage of this statement to his vulnerable core.

He waited, but no obvious threat revealed itself, and he began to let the words pass through him, though ready to seal off the untraversed layers if these words inflicted any unexpected injury. This was the last thing he would imagine to hear from Alexander. Lucas almost forgot he still remained in a social dynamic, but his conditioning urged a reply.

With all the confidence he could muster to conceal his doubt, Lucas gave thanks and decided the best way to maintain his hold on the situation was to allow a certain degree of transparency, to allow some of the internal to manifest in the external. "I was not expecting to hear that from you. I'll try to take that to heart."

"Anytime." Alexander said as he lit the freshly rolled cigarette. He took a few puffs, then offered it to Lucas. "Want a hit?"

Thinking that lowering his barriers with this person merited a ceremonial communion, Lucas accepted the cigarette saying "I have never smoked a hand rolled cigarette before, so I suppose I should take this opportunity." Lucas brought the cigarette to his lips, and as he inhaled, he sensed the true beginning of the bond germinating between them. He pondered what would come of their meeting and why he was doing this, but no answer came. In the silence, Lucas felt a pulling on his being. The decision seemed made for him already. He must continue.

"This is a good moment." Lucas said. "I feel really good here in this time and space." Lucas returned the cigarette.

"Yeah, man. I know just what you mean." A bright glow illuminated from the red ember of the burning cigarette as Alexander intensified his suction.

Lucas could not help losing himself in that glow. The manifold processes and energy exchanges taking place. The thermal energy agitating the atoms and molecules causing bonds to break and a destruction and transformation of the components in the paper and tobacco. The gaseous products, then, traveling into the orifice Alexander exposed and flowing to his lungs to diffuse into the blood stream. Lucas imagined the nicotine spreading through Alexander's body reacting with the acetylcholine receptors throughout his musculature, then, diffusing, again, past the blood-brain barrier and eliciting its cascading effects therein.

Lucas thought: *Like all these processes here before me, our lives, too, play their role in a chain of events, but how could we possibly fathom the larger picture?*

"So, do you want to see that street I was talking about?" Alexander asked. He flicked the cigarette butt off a side of the ledge.

"Yeah, that sounds good."

Getting down never occurred to Lucas. His focus had been so fixated on the present, he forgot about the future. As he realized getting down may be just as dangerous as climbing up, fear washed over him once more.

He watched as Alexander hung off the ledge directly above the step below and dropped onto it. Alexander leaped forward again using one foot, this time his left, to push himself off the wall between the steps and propel him the rest of the way. He, then, lowered himself to the step below. Once there, he sat with his legs dangling, slid off the step landing on the slopping wall, and ran to the bottom.

Lucas followed dropping down to the first step. Then, he realized the jump he avoided earlier was now unavoidable. "Whoops. I guess I have to jump." Lucas felt himself tremble, but shortly, energy burst into his limbs. He soared to the midpoint, kicked off the wall, and landed on the other step. Lucas descended from that point on with ease, confidence, and a sudden surge of strength. As he ran down, he intoned "Oh, yeah!"

"Great job!" Alexander said with a smile.

"Thanks." Lucas dusted himself off, then turned to Alexander. "So, let's get going."

They hopped the fences again and trekked the upward slope of the park towards parking lot.

"Hey do you want to try my backpack on, see what it's like?"

"Sure, why not?" Lucas attempted to hide his swelling excitement.

Alexander slipped off his backpack and handed it off to Lucas, who immediately swung it around one shoulder and caught it with the other arm. Lucas felt surprised by the heaviness of the backpack and could feel his leg and back muscles compensating for the extra weight. His enthusiasm transformed as his character shifted and became the enthusiasm of an adventurer about to embark on a much anticipated sojourn. He marched onward.

"We'll need to get on the train and ride for about twenty minutes."

They walked a few blocks and stopped at a city train station. Benches were placed in equal intervals along the platform. Alexander sat down, and after removing the backpack, Lucas joined him.

"Do you believe in multiple dimensions?" asked Alexander.

Lucas shuffled in his seat accentuating the surprise he felt. "Do you mean like multiple universes?"

"Kind of. We live in a three dimensional world. The fourth dimension is time, but the fifth dimension is more significant to me because the fifth dimension holds the multiple possible outcomes of the fourth dimension. Our paths are influenced by our decisions and by chance, and depending on our choices, we have multiple possible futures. Once we make a choice, one future occurs, and all other possibilities no longer exist for us. There's more dimensions, but these are all I focus on. Do you remember the die I have?"

"The wooden one?"

"Yeah, so the other night I rolled it, and it landed on five. For me five means something to do with my fate. I rolled it because I was unsure if I should sleep next to the edge of that shelf at my home. The five told me I needed to reconsider my choice because something big was going to happen, so I decided not to sleep at the edge. I guarantee that in another dimensional outcome, I died that night. Probably, rolled off the side in my sleep."

"Wow, I never thought about that. I think I understand. So, do you think we really have control over our future?"

The train pulled up to the station, and they rose to meet it as the doors opened. Alexander grabbed his backpack and led the way, circumnavigating the people standing or searching for available seats. Lucas focused on following Alexander and avoiding collisions with the people he passed. Alexander chose a section that had four seats, two sides facing each other with two seats each. He placed the backpack in one seat and sat in the other while Lucas sprawled out on the two adjoining seats opposite of him. The doors closed, and a sudden jerk indicated the train's departure. Lucas suddenly realized they did not purchase tickets.

"We have some control over our future." Alexander continued. "The choices we make are what give us control, but we can't control everything. Our circumstances are determined for us, at least initially. Then, we get to move about possible paths that have already been created. The control we have is the ability to choose which path we take. I don't think we get to create the path though. In every moment, there are an infinite number of doors and paths beyond, but these have already been created. We just get to walk the path we choose, and once we choose, that's the only path."

"That makes sense if you look at it within the frame of reference that we are products of existence and not creators of it. You have to think of us as builders or artists. We create things with the material available to us, the material already created. What we create are merely possible products predetermined by our material and our cognitive capacities, thus we don't have absolute control of what we create. In order to have complete control, we would need to have the ability to create the raw materials and our cognitive capacities. We would need to be able to create matter and energy. We would have to be gods."

"Exactly! We can't be products and be creators. A product can't create itself, and a creator can't be created."

Lucas observed the people in the train car. Written on the majority of faces was an expression of weariness. In each of those eyes lay defeat. These people were broken. One exception, however, caught Lucas' attention, a man and his twelve year old son. They spoke to one another with love in their eyes and smiles undiminished by the formation of words. A sense of longing began to swell inside, but Lucas diverted his attention back to Alexander.

"You have to be careful when you make that point." Lucas cautioned. That relies completely on the human ability to perceive the universe. We see things in terms of cause and effect; for one effect to occur another must precede it. So, when you say a creator cannot be created, you draw from this logical foundation. The way we developed this logic was by, aside from evolving the necessary cognitive capacities, observing the seemingly linear progression of moment to moment.

"The acts of the present influence or cause the acts of the future. Then, we thought if this line goes 'forward,' then it must also go backward. We began to understand how past effects caused present effects. We realized a logical structure in which every layer is a cause and an effect simultaneously, however, we retained the notion that there must be a point of origin, the creator.

"But, what if this linear way of thought is incorrect? What if cause and effect do not function the way we understand them to? Then, your point falls apart, and we are left, once again, in the unknown."

"You have a point there, man, but I can't imagine any other way of thinking."

"I don't know if we can due to the limitations of our cognitive capacities, however, some different ideas have been presented. For instance, the idea that the universe was never created but always existed. That attempts to eliminate the cause and effect element from the 'origin' by eliminating the origin itself, but this doesn't quite make sense if we maintain that cause and effect exist. If we remove this element from the origin, we would then need to eliminate it from every aspect of existence. If the universe always existed, then there are no long tendrils of cause and effect running through existence.

"I think this because if there was no origin of the universe, then cause and effect would need to have been created at some point, but this would be an act of creation within an already existent universe. We already agreed we can't create raw materials, and I think this includes the laws governing the reactions that birth the tendrils of cause and effect. Furthermore, I assume that nothing in existence can create existence. If this is the case, then the tendrils of cause and effect could only have been created in the 'origin' of the universe, which leads us back to a point in which it was created. Again, this takes us in a circle. It seems like we have to abandon the notion of cause and effect in order for that theory to work, at least according to human logic."

"Or, we have to abandon our concept of time."

"What do you mean?"

"Cause and effect are labeled according to which came before or after. We use time to determine what is cause and what is effect. Time exists in the fourth dimension, but we only see three dimensional cross sections of time, what we call moments, because we are three dimensional beings that can only see in three dimensions. The passage of time is an illusion, so maybe cause and effect are illusions as well. Maybe, things just are and are not determined by anything already in existence."

"But, that contradicts what you said earlier about our choice determining our future."

"Unless, we don't actually have choices. What if choices are only cross sectional views of a larger dimension, and there are no choices because all possibilities exists?"

"But we have finite outcomes in our lives. I can't be the me I am now and be some other me, like a famous scientist."

"Well, only if you think of yourself as you are here as the complete you. I think we are only cross sections of ourselves and that we exist, that everything exists in all the higher dimensions. The highest dimension, maybe the tenth, is the complete form of existence, and all lower dimensions are just parts of it. That means the complete us, whatever that may be, is composed of all the parts of the lower dimensions. These parts are what we think of as possibilities, except, these are not things that could be but things that are. So, choices are illusions because only one existence exists."

"That sounds like predestination, but with that frame of reference, predestination would also be an illusion, or misperception. For predestination to exist multiple paths would need to exist, but in your perspective the infinite possible paths are merely cross sections of one path, and only one path exists."

"One infinitely divisible path." Alexander added.

Lucas glanced back at the defeated faces and the father and son. Applying this novel idea, Lucas began imagining different possible states for the people surrounding him. He tried to imagine them happy, talking to one another, sharing precious memories from their lives, and giving love and acceptance to all.

Then, he imagined them with expressionless faces staring blankly into nothingness. Each possessing a device protruding from the neck that directly integrated in to the brain controlling its functions. Mindless, these people had become or were created. They rode the train home from the factory where they assembled more devices to be attached to the newborns and those being assimilated. The father and son sat silently next to each other, did not acknowledge the other's presence, maybe not even their own.

Lucas realized these two imagined possibilities and the one he currently resided in all existed, at least within this new frame of reference. Each possibility was simply a cross-section of the whole. He wandered what that whole could be, a whole composed of contradictory parts. Perhaps, contradiction, too, must be abandoned.

"This frame of reference requires us to abandon a great many *truths*, many ways of perception that we take for granted under the title of common sense." Lucas returned his gaze back to Alexander but could not rid the lost expression on his face. "This conversation turns logic upside down, removes any sort of foundation we thought we were standing on."

"Yeah, it makes you wonder if there is any true foundation or direction for logic."

"I used to strongly believe so. I knew what up and down were, but recently, I realized if you go down far enough, you start going up. It seems limiting perception to directions and foundations is detrimental to our understanding. Perhaps, we prematurely draw conclusions and label things as truth."

"Good possibility, man."

The train jerked to a stop. Alexander motioned for them to disembark. They brushed past the other passengers and stepped off the train on the other side of the downtown area.

The temperature had fallen a couple degrees, and the breeze picked up speed. The wind squeezed into every crack and cranny of their clothes in a cool embrace. Lucas looked at the sky and raised his arms to the stars above, opening himself further to the wind's caress. Alexander took notice and did the same, but he could not resist the urge to howl. Lucas grinned and joined in.

The many eyes in the vicinity eagerly searched these two for answers to unanswerable questions. Surely, such an oddity as this must bring with it a wisdom of great illumination, but no eye hinted at discovery. Only frustration permeated them.

With a heavy but relaxed sigh, Lucas lowered his arms and began walking to the nearest sidewalk. Alexander, reluctant to pass this moment, lingered for a second then followed and took the lead once more by Lucas' side.

"So," Lucas began, "if we are only one cross section of many, do we have a permanent fixture, or can we flow from one cross section to another?"

"I think that's what the illusion of choice is. The transition from one cross section to another. If we couldn't move about, then we would be parts completely divided from the whole, however, I think we are the parts and the whole. As parts, we are never truly separated from the whole, so we can become different parts. Another way to look at it is we are all the parts, though we can only experience them one at a time. That includes time travel, man!"

"And so, we can *choose* which cross-section we want to be."

"Yeah, and we can be anything because we are everything."

"We are infinity!" Lucas jumped slightly from the shock of this epiphany. A touch of warmth centered on his chest and relief washed over him as he realized he could be anything, is everything. He continued.

"That means the entire universe is infinity, and all things can be every one of their possible expressions, are every one of them. We simply have to flow towards the cross-sections we want to experience. Civilization can be anything, and it is what we choose it to be. Our relationship with nature can be anything, but we have chosen to forsake a healthy one. Life could be all the more beautiful, but we condemn ourselves to only this sliver. If we can be anything, why do we limit ourselves to this?" Lucas gestured to the skyscrapers surrounding them. "There are infinite possible expressions of beauty!"

"Now, that is the million dollar question. I know I would never create this, at least not the way it is now. Instead of separating ourselves from nature, I would bring civilization to nature in a harmonious way. We wouldn't destroy ecosystems and drive species unnecessarily to extinction. The air we would breathe would be fresh, pollution free. The water completely clean. We would respect the laws of nature. We wouldn't overpopulate. We would live simply and in harmony with all species, not dominating them. We would have humility and respect for all things. We would act with the understanding that everything is one and with love for all things.

"We could have houses made in trees. I mean the insides of the trees themselves would be genetically designed to form a house, and as the tree grew, the house would grow too. Yeah, we would have science as developed as it is now, but it would be integrated into our harmonious lifestyle. We don't need to separate ourselves completely from nature to have advancements in science, and if we do, I don't think those advances would be worth it.

"We would learn how to communicate with all species of life and the rest of the world. We would be a global community of life and planet working together to create a better, more beautiful world. Everyone and everything would take care of each other. Food wouldn't be a problem, because all species would understand their place on the food web and would willing give themselves to their consumers. Consumers would only consume what they need, nothing more. Nothing would fear death, because death wouldn't exist, only a transformation of one form of the universe to another.

"Also, domestication wouldn't exist for any creature, plant, animal, or human. Everything will have the freedom to express itself comfortably with no lamentations. We wouldn't compare ourselves but admire each other's differences. We would realize that everything is great and powerful, and this would reflect in our interactions with everyone and everything. People need to start calling each other beautiful, because we don't hear enough of that!"

At that moment, a man dressed in a suit walked swiftly past, purpose emanating from him. As he passed, Alexander said warmly and smoothly "Hey, man. You're beautiful. Don't let anybody tell you different." The man replied with a grin and a nod and continued on his way.

"One more thing; no one would be forced to pick a *career* to be stuck in for the rest of their lives. That's just ridiculous! We are constantly changing. People would have the ability to move from profession to profession to find their calling or find their new calling. Along with that, children would be asked more about their dreams and how they will achieve them, but this wouldn't stop once the children became adults. We would ask each other constantly at any age and encourage each other to fulfill them. Ninety year olds would be asked, and of course, they have dreams!"

The energy of Alexander's last statement brought a smile to Lucas' face, and he could not hold back his thoughts any longer. "Yeah, that sounds exactly like how I would create civilization, though I want to add the dismantling of the social hierarchy or the absence of it. I think this is included in the absence of domestication, but I want to accentuate it. Instead of thinking of our differences on a vertical plane, we would see them on a horizontal plane. Of course, we wouldn't think of ourselves as equals in the sense that we are the same, rather we are equal in the sense that we all have a role to play in existence, that we exist. To hold one's existence over another's is baseless bias. We cannot possibly fathom any true hierarchy if one does in fact exist. That awareness lies beyond our capabilities since we only experience parts of the whole.

"This notion applied to our social structure would eradicate any form of superiority. People will simply fulfill what role they play. In order to assure this, great study of methods that illuminate most clearly what our roles are would be conducted, but the ultimate decision will reside with the individual. Like you mentioned earlier about professions, there would be fluidity granted to us to discover our true role and any changes occurring throughout our lives.

"The incentives driving people towards progress would no longer need to rely on wealth, prestige, power, security, acceptance, the threat of losing love and happiness; any and all manifestations of fear. People would not have to compete with one another to affirm their existence. Instead, people's existence will already be affirmed. They would have every need met simply because they exist. The drive towards progress would be fueled not by fulfilling basic needs but by the deep desire to achieve the fullest expression of our existence, to grow in ways that matter.

"What I speak of has nothing to do with population, control over nature, nor control over other people. No, I speak of striving to become the next form of Homo sapiens, striving to evolve within the natural order of things, to expand our cognitive capacities and our understanding of existence without attempting to separate ourselves from the rest of the universe. And, producing the finest of thoughts and their products along the way to finer thoughts and products."

The street they sought appeared just ahead about a block away. People laid with their heads adjacent to or sat against a brick wall barring those on the sidewalk from getting too close to the building contained within. Many people used flattened cardboard boxes as palates, or they simply made due with the concrete sidewalk.

Realizing what they approached, Lucas broke away from the flow of conversation asking "Is this the street you were talking about?"

"Yup, that's it."

Upon reaching the crosswalk, Lucas noticed the larger number homeless people completely occupying the two visible sides of the square block. As they crossed, Lucas felt the sudden sting of reality. Before him lay human beings living without the basic necessities readily available to him and most. He looked into the eyes of those awake and tried to find some oddity within, something to make them not quite human. Desperate, he darted his eyes from one subject to another only to feel the desperation intensify. Finding no help from those wide-eyes staring back at him, Lucas shifted his attention to the sleeping bodies. Perhaps, he reasoned, the abnormality reveals itself when they slept.

He noticed how some used their shoes as pillows for either comfort or to protect them from thieves, maybe both. Given the warmer temperature, blankets were quite unnecessary, and because of this, Lucas was offered more to study. The clothing worn, though in some cases tattered, looked remarkably normal. Many were clean shaven and had clean-cut hair. If Lucas were to pass these people on the street, he would see no outward indication of their homelessness.

Lucas realized that uncovering any accurate peculiarities could not be achieved from the exterior alone. No outward appearance denoted any deviation from humanity. These people looked human, but he pressed on thinking there must be something within if anything at all, however, now was not the time to investigate. Lucas suspended the thought placing it in the proper compartment to be explored and applied at another time.

Lucas remained silently studying the individuals sprawled out on the ground trying not to think but observe. Alexander sensed the importance of his leadership now more than ever and made sure to guide Lucas as he focused on the spectacle before him. Alexander chose to walk the full perimeter of the square block to allow Lucas as much time and subjects as possible. Alexander, also aware of the obvious innocence on Lucas' face and the danger that invited, adopted the most confident and assured air he could to insure any threats would think twice before approaching. The baseball bat sticking out of his bag did wonders for his cause.

They returned to where they started without Lucas noticing, and he jumped a little once he realized his position. Alexander asked "Did you see enough?"

"Yes, I think I saw enough, for now."

Allowing Lucas to remain deep in thought, Alexander led the way across the street heading towards the courtyard of a church. The courtyard measured about a hundred feet long and fifty feet wide surrounded by a metal fence reaching four feet in height. The only way in was to climb the fence.

Lucas hardly noticed where they headed nor Alexander approaching the fence. With a fluid motion, Alexander lifted himself up and swung himself over the top of the fence. Lucas simply followed with very little thought. Alexander walked toward a wooden patio table with complementary chairs displaced and scattered about. Lucas sat down watching Alexander rearrange the chairs to a more orderly arrangement.

Once Alexander finished, Lucas asked "Why did you do that?"

Alexander shrugged and sat down explaining "better vibes this way." He grabbed another cigarette and lit it.

Confused but contented, Lucas let the matter go. Instead, he commented on the courtyard "This place is pretty cool. It's relaxing and beautiful. A great escape from the city."

Alexander nodded as he inhaled. "This is one of my favorite spots. The vibes here are great," he said on the exhale, smoke dancing from his mouth as he spoke.

Lucas started abruptly "Those people looked normal. Maybe, a little ragged, but normal. I couldn't see any indication of any sort of abnormality that would render them less than human, nothing that should cast them to the bottom of our social hierarchy."

"Well, yeah man. They're people." Alexander said playfully.

Lucas stood up and a little exasperatedly responded "I know that!" Lucas paced back and forth in front of the table as he spoke. "I'm looking for any vestige of proof that justifies their placement on the social hierarchy. There were no visible signs, at least with that particular group, but this only makes me want to dig deeper."

"And, how do you want to do that?" Alexander asked as he leaned forward drawn by Lucas' energy.

Still pacing to better crank out his thoughts, Lucas answered "I suppose talking is the next step, see if there are any psychological problems that present themselves. Other than that, I'm not sure."

"Do you want to talk to them now?"

"No, not tonight." Before Lucas could finish, a beam of light shined on them from outside the courtyard. Both quickly looked to identify the source. At the fence where they climbed stood a police officer with his very bright flash light.

A deep voice roared "This is private property. You can't be here!"

Lucas froze not knowing what to do nor what was going to happen. A shudder of fear ran through him, but he swallowed it down. If Alexander was not with him, Lucas would have stared blankly at the officer for an eternity.

"Oh, this is?" asked Alexander innocently. "I didn't know."

Lucas turned to the police officer anticipating a deafening roar. He struggled to quiet the screams in his head.

The officer gave no sign of belief or disbelief but answered "Yes it is, you need to leave."

"Okay, no problem." Alexander said calmly as he rose from his seat. Lucas, already standing, waited for Alexander to lead the way.

He decided he would observe and remain silent.

They climbed back over the fence, and Alexander addressed the officer again. "This is one of my favorite spots because of how peaceful it is."

The officer appeared to have heard Alexander, but his mind had already assumed the course of the conversation. He replied unconcerned for Alexander's divergence "I'm just doing my job. This is the church's courtyard, and if I don't keep you out, I'd lose my job. If it were up to me, I'd let you stay. It's not me."

Lucas noted the extreme defensiveness that overcame the officer. The officer made short jerky gestures and even seemed to tremble a little. Lucas knew the officer could not be afraid of a physical confrontation. After all, he was larger than Lucas and Alexander combined. No, Lucas realized the officer was not struggling with a fear of the two young men in front of him, rather he struggled with the fear that accompanies any confrontation with humanity. Here, the officer was forcing himself to execute laws he did not believe in. The internal war revealed itself in every word uttered and movement made.

"Oh, yeah man. I get that you are just doing your job. I'm just saying how great this place is."

The officer replied again but spoke to neither Alexander nor Lucas but to an unseen judge. "I wouldn't kick you out if it were up to me. It's the church that doesn't want people here at night. I just have to do my job."

Lucas felt annoyed by the officer's indirect address but remained silent and blank-faced. Alexander understood that the police officer was in no position to have a real conversation, so he gave up and said "No problem. We'll just get out of here."

Together, all three walked the length of the pathway leading to the sidewalk. When they reached the sidewalk, Lucas and Alexander turned right heading back towards the street flocked with the homeless, as the officer crossed the street to his car.

After a while, Lucas broke the silence "Well, that was interesting. Freaked me out a little, but not too bad. I didn't like how the officer talked to us or rather at us. It seemed like he talked to some sort of higher force or power like God or mortality or destiny itself."

"Yeah, people do that when they fear what they are doing. He knew deep down that this system of protection isn't actually needed.

He knew that the problem didn't lie with us but those who betray the efforts of humanity, and these people don't have to exist. They exist because humanity isn't taking care of itself. Humanity is in the middle of denial, and it shows in times like these."

Lucas reflected on what Alexander said. He never thought of individuals acting on behalf of humanity as a whole. This new perspective intrigued him as he imagined individuals playing the role of antibodies in humanity's immune system. Lucas pictured the police officer as an antibody denying its programming to isolate antigens, and instead, in a tragic misdirection, attacking the organism itself. He began to see governments and any form of control over others as symptoms of this greater autoimmune disease.

Lucas imagined that a healthy system would correct the individual problems at their point of origin, completely eradicating all threats and thus the need for antibodies. Humanity as he saw it, however, seemed to be mass producing antibodies to attack humanity as a whole to compensate for its inability to deal directly with specific threats. Lucas thought if people would spend more time trying to truly solve humanity's problems at their source, then there would be no need for governments or anyone or anything in power. Lucas realized this could only come to fruition when humanity is ready to see itself in its entirety, its capabilities and limitations, a true transparency. Humanity merely needs to open its eyes. A sadness seized him.

"I don't understand why it has to be this way. All we need to do is decide to change our ways. Why do we run away?" Lucas looked desperately at Alexander imploring him to provide all the missing pieces to this enigma and lay it clearly before him.

Alexander recognized the import of those hungry eyes peering into his, but he knew he could not satiate this dire hunger. He looked at his feet feeling he was letting Lucas down. "I don't know." he replied grimly.

"It doesn't make sense!" Lucas shouted. "The solution is so simple. All we need to do is look within for the knowledge to help others, to eradicate heinous acts with graceful love and understanding. Humanity has turned on itself, and it seems the only outcome is our annihilation!"

Lucas surprised Alexander when he turned back towards him not caring to conceal the tears beginning to form in the corners of his eyes. Alexander never took this matter as personally as Lucas did in this moment. He wondered now how someone could care this much. Life had been a ride for Alexander, nothing more than a ride. Sure, he considered every action to be significant and life to be important, but he never internalized his experience quite so much. He always felt like a spectator, someone outside of existence. Here before him was a glimpse of another degree of existing, a truer attunement to existence, and his focus gravitated to the vehement figure.

"There will come a time when we won't be able to run anymore. What will happen then? Will we change or be destroyed? If we know our ways are unsustainable, let's not wait for a critical moment to push us in the right direction. Let's circumvent this trajectory, now, before we have to! We need to live proactively not reactively."

"Yeah, I agree, but that requires the impossible. People need to have the courage to look at themselves."

"It's not impossible, damn it! What makes it impossible is people immediately thinking 'oh, that's impossible' whenever they encounter this idea. If we stopped caring solely about the immediate effects of our attempts to understand ourselves and our subsequent actions, we would accomplish a lot more. Instead of focusing on instantly gratifying ourselves, we need to commit to our realizations and become catalyst for change. If we change nothing now, at least we carry the torch of our revelations for the next generation. Change fails to occur when people simply give up."

"You're right! All people need to do is allow this change to happen." Alexander straightened as the magnitude of this realization began to settle. "Like you said, *change* is going to happen. That much is inevitable. The only thing stopping change from happening now is us. We are denying lessons learned like stubborn children."

Lucas nodded eagerly then added "that's what infuriates me. Change itself is simple; getting people to allow it is a monumental task. That just seems absurd to me! Change should only be difficult in itself, not because all these people wish to cling to older, dead ideas."

"How do you get people to allow change then?"

"You don't, as far as I know. You just have to change yourself. When they see you are still alive and well, they will begin to loosen their grip on those dead ideas. They will never let go completely until they embrace the change themselves, however, it takes a long time for people to become desensitized to their fears. A long time, sometimes, too long."

"Yeah man, I agree with that!" Alexander lifted his hand and pointed. "Let's go that way."

Lucas did not see the intersection they approached. He almost stumbled off the curb where the sidewalk met the street. In the direction Alexander had pointed, he recognized the square block orbited by the homeless and felt himself oddly pulled to it as well. His internal compass nudged him again, but he could not understand why it directed him thus. Though, he never did.

Again, they crossed disregarding the system created solely for this purpose. Lucas let Alexander lead the way and thought he always would for these occasions. Alexander gave no sign of concern and happily and proudly took the lead, swaggering in that smooth fashion of his. Lucas felt something in Alexander, especially at times like these, that he himself needed in order to take the next step in life's progression.

Alexander was more eager to sit than observe his surroundings, so he dashed straight for an opening on the sidewalk. Lucas followed unquestioningly, simply pursuing that amorphous substance emanating from his companion. Quickly, another hole in the mass of people was filled.

The exhaustion on Alexander's face finally penetrated Lucas' sensory perception as he watched Alexander yawn and lean his head back, so Lucas decided to allow Alexander to direct the conversation.

After a long pause, Alexander spoke. "Do you have a phone I can use to message some friends and family? I won't take long."

A little surprised by the request but recovering well, Lucas replied "Yeah, sure," and handed him the phone from his pocket. Lucas had not yet thought about how Alexander's circumstance isolated him from his friends and family. He did not even consider that Alexander had any to contact and felt a little ashamed of his shortsightedness and naivety.

"Thanks, man! I haven't messaged them in a while." Alexander accepted the phone, and once he found the Facebook application, began typing away.

Lucas sat observing the people around him. To his left, a man in nice looking clothes, hardly an indication of his status, lay on a flattened piece of cardboard. Under his head, the cardboard humped over a pair of shoes.

Lucas' eyes darted to Alexander at his right as he remembered his existence. To Lucas, Alexander appeared to be a normal young man engrossed in a device most took for granted. He wondered how someone lacking the most basic of necessities could appear so normal, so unperturbed. Perhaps, this was what was missing from him.

A group of three men walked up to the both of them, and one asked "Does that phone work?"

Fear gripped Lucas, and he wisely remained silent. Alexander, however, as coolly as ever, responded almost immediately.

"No, this phone doesn't have service. I'm just writing some poetry."

The man responded just as quickly "Does it have Wi-Fi?"

Lucas imagined the discourse before him to resemble two bears standing as tall as they could to intimidate the other. One sought the resource of the other, and the other merely wanted to protect his access.

Quick to the draw again, Alexander replied "Yeah, it has internet when it connects to Wi-Fi, but there's no Wi-Fi here." Lucas felt extremely grateful to have Alexander by his side, and he noticed a protective expression on Alexander's face.

The man watched as Alexander returned his attention to the phone and studied the nonchalant nature he presented. The man could find no holes in this façade. He decided not to push the matter further afraid of what was really at risk. "Alright," he concluded and walked away.

Lucas used everything in his power to conceal his growing fright, but when the man turned the corner, he could hide it no longer. "Wow, what the hell was that? I'm glad you could handle it."

Alexander just shrugged as he kept typing.

A few minutes later, Alexander looked up from the phone and handed it back to Lucas. "Thanks, man."

"No problem." Lucas retrieved his phone and replaced it into his pocket. As he did so, he read the time. "I need to go soon. It's getting late."

"Yeah, man. It's all good. It was cool meeting you. I haven't had this good of conversation in a while." Lucas could have sworn he saw disappointment show on Alexander's face as he spoke.

"I'm not finished experiencing the streets. I'd like to join you sometime soon and actually stay a few days. Would you be up to that?" Lucas withheld a grin when he saw Alexander's subtle disappointment suddenly turn to excitement. Of course, Lucas could only speculate that this was what that tiny twitch at the corner of Alexander's mouth meant. To say for certain was impossible while Alexander maintained such a serene persona.

"Definitely. We can schedule something. Add me on Facebook and message me when you want to start. I'll find a way to check it."

Again, that nonchalant attitude infected Lucas with an eager desire for that essence, and Alexander's access to the internet intrigued him further. His eagerness radiated as he hurriedly replied "Alright!" Lucas pulled out his phone again, reopened the appropriate application, and handed Alexander the phone. "Can you add yourself for me?"

"Sure thing." Alexander took the phone and began the process.

Lucas tapped his feet and twisted in place. "This is going to be awesome! This will be an experience of a lifetime, and I'm going to learn so much. I just know it."

"Yeah, man. I look forward to it." Alexander looked up with amusement as he held out Lucas' phone. "It will definitely be a journey."

Lucas retrieved his phone and shook Alexander's hand. "I'll be in touch with you soon. Very soon. Are you staying here tonight?"

"Sure am. I'll check my messages regularly. Have a goodnight, man."

"You too! See you soon." Lucas held eye contact for a long moment then nodded and walked in the direction he thought his car was located. *This is what I've been waiting for!*

THE JOURNEY

Today was the day. Lucas had everything packed and ready to go. Thankfully, Alexander had given Lucas a list of all the necessities which made packing all the easier, and Lucas made sure to follow it completely. He had two of every clothing article: shirts, pants, socks, underwear, and shoes. He also packed his toothbrush, toothpaste, hand sanitizer, two water bottles, two blankets, a sheet, a pillow, string, rope, pens, paper, a pocket knife, and a wooden pole to serve as a club. Alexander had stressed bringing some form of protection.

Two conditions were agreed upon: Lucas must leave his money at home and could only bring his cell phone as long as it remained off. Lucas felt these conditions added to the excitement, so he readily accepted them. He was tempted to even leave his phone, but he finally concluded he needed a contingency plan. In place of money, Lucas would bring his djembe and Alexander a newly acquired guitar, and together, they would street perform for sustenance. It seemed a sound enough plan to Lucas, though he was not sure he knew what sound was anymore.

They would spend four days and four nights together starting on a Wednesday night and ending sometime Sunday. There was no further plan. They were just going to "follow the good vibes" as Alexander put it. Lucas, of course, had no idea what that meant but was eager to find out. Lucas assumed they would sleep at Alexander's home under the bridge well shielded from curious eyes and the eyes that brought trouble, but Lucas wanted to stray from the safety of that home and venture into the mysterious streets to discover what they had in store for them.

Lucas was taking only a backpack and his djembe, which rested on the wall nearest his bedroom door. On top of his backpack, Lucas had tethered his nicely rolled blankets, sheets, and pillow like Alexander demonstrated a few days prior. The wooden pole was placed between the roll and the backpack secured by the tension of the rope. Although Lucas was absent, an unmistakable kinetic energy suffused his bedroom. The inanimate appeared animate.

This ambient energy stirred even more as Lucas stampeded through the doorway, threw on his backpack, picked up his djembe, and exited just as swiftly. Lucas nearly ran out the front door of his house straight to his father's beige SUV. Quickly, he placed his backpack in the trunk, and with a loud slam, Lucas closed the trunk and rushed to the passenger seat. Another slam, and Lucas was buckled up and ready to go with his djembe between his knees.

To his annoyance, Lucas' father walked at an immeasurably slow pace driving Lucas to the brink of shouting to hurry. Somehow, he managed to hold back his vehement command with the tapping of his fingers on his thigh, and the tapping intensified as his father entered the vehicle. Relief collided with anxiety creating an even more tempestuous feeling as Lucas realized he was one step closer to his sojourn. Anticipation had haunted him for three weeks since he and Alexander had arranged a date and time of departure.

To kick off their adventure, Alexander requested that Lucas help him make a dream come true. Alexander wanted to perform with Lucas at his favorite bar which had an open mic on Wednesday nights and welcomed the misfits of the night. Lucas, eager to maximize his adventure, agreed enthusiastically. He, too, dreamed of performing on stage, and he could not think of a more fitting way to jump into the unknown. He was afraid, but he was going to fear in style. And so, as they drove to their designated rendezvous, Lucas played his djembe to the radio.

Once they neared their destination, Lucas directed his father to a parking lot most accommodating to their threshold for walking which just so happened to be the L-shaped parking lot across from Alexander's home. After retrieving his backpack, Lucas rejoined his father and led the way to what he knew could only be a trans-dimensional door whose sole purpose was to usher him to a completely novel state of being. The hairs on the back of his neck began to stand as the venue came into view. Some powerful energy flowed through the universe awe-inspiringly perceptible to Lucas, and a tremor convulsed through him. The transformation had already begun.

They entered the scarcely populated bar practically unnoticed, but Alexander, already seated, let out a great howl in their direction. The howl, quite impossible to ignore, attracted the many darting eyes of that few. Lucas had come too far to back down now, so he inhaled deeply and let out a quaking roar of a howl. Realizing a legitimate language was being spoken, the curious eyes shifted back to their musings unperturbed.

"Hey, man!" Alexander shouted as he paced towards Lucas and his father. "You ready?"

Lucas reached to embrace Alexander's hand. "Hell yeah I am! Are you?"

"Of course, I am. Is this your dad?"

"Yup. Alexander meet Dad. Dad meet Alexander."

"Nice to meet you sir." Alexander gestured for a handshake.

A little awkwardly, Lucas' father shook Alexander's hand. "Nice to meet you, too."

Alexander guided them to the seats he had already claimed. Close by, on the floor, Alexander's bag and guitar leaned against a bench. He gestured for Lucas to do the same with his things, and they all sat down together.

Lucas could not help showing his nervousness as he asked "So, when do we go on tonight?"

As smoothly as ever Alexander answered "I signed us up as number fourteen. If nobody bails, then that's when we go. If someone does, we go sooner."

This eased Lucas a little. With the number of performances preceding him, Lucas felt he would have ample precedent to cushion his emergence on stage. "Sounds good. Gives me some time to see what I'm getting myself into."

There, they sat talking about one another, the bar, and the performances. Most of the acts were poets sharing multitudes of poems on topics ranging from sex, relationships, women's rights, and even defecation. A few two-person bands played, dividing themselves into guitar and various forms of percussion; some combined their efforts on guitar. There was one rapper "spitten rhymes from his prime." Each performance brought an atmosphere of its own, taking everyone present along an undulating ride rich with the potential for losing oneself. At least, Lucas did. His bearings seemed to be ripped from him as though an ethereal hand reached inside and tore out the very sensory basis of his perception.

Before he knew it, the thirteenth expression concluded, and his own turn, now, beckoned him to position himself at Alexander's side on the stage. As he watched Alexander rise, Lucas' heart began to pull him to his feet with each thumping beat. He jumped up feeling purpose course through him inflating his limbs. His nervousness, however, had long left, and all that remained was the ineffable happening of a potentiality realizing itself. Lucas grabbed his djembe and followed Alexander to the stage.

Both awkwardly groped their way about, stepping around equipment and props and over wires. Finally, they found their way to the center. Alexander sat on a wooden stool, while Lucas made do with a small, square ottoman. The sound engineer strategically placed microphones around them. As the sound engineer retreated, Alexander and Lucas locked eyes, nodded slightly, faced the crowd, tilted up their heads, and howled. The entire crowd, adamant about supporting their brethren, sent a reverberating howl in reply.

After a second's pregnant pause Lucas slammed down on his djembe sounding the beginning of their opening song, an Alexander original. Alexander joined in and began singing. They had rehearsed only once a few days before, but at the moment, no one could possibly tell. Alexander strummed away, and Lucas somehow managed to keep up with Alexander's sporadic and unpredictable timing changes. The tempo rose and fell. The beat count shifted slightly. Lucas hung on to that wave of musical cognizance for dear life but felt it slipping away. He did not know how long he would be able to maintain.

Then, the first song came to an end, and the crowd cheered and clapped. Immediately, they began the next. This one they covered, and of all of them, this would be the most challenging. The tempo was slightly faster, yet still remained at a steady, mellow pace. They chose the order of their songs, so that each would build the energy gradually, ending with a bang.

Alexander had struggled especially with this song when they rehearsed, and the struggle made itself obvious this night as well. Great concentration showed on his face as he progressed from verse to chorus and then, back again. His voice faltered a little, but his recovery masked it well. His knack for making chaotic timing changes flow helped immensely when his fingers resisted a command. His stumble appeared apart of the show.

Lucas ground his teeth as he forced all his creative power into a burst of recovery accents leading back to as steady a rhythm as Alexander's playing allowed. Lucas looked up from his drum and surveyed the audience. The recovery seemed to be accepted, at least, if not truly pulled off. A few faces formed expressions of constrained understanding, but the overall consensus, Lucas discerned, was of positive regard. Now, was no time to give up.

After the second song ended, the third began. Another Alexander original. The energy despite the rough execution of the last song, never faded and began to rise even further. This song had a Blues feel to it, though slightly variant and was, relatively speaking, performed perfectly. The crowd felt compelled to clap along, Alexander and Lucas radiated with joy.

Another applause, and the grand finale initiated the climax of their performance. This Indie song had the fastest tempo and most moving rhythm of those preceding. The captivated audience cheered with encouragement and surprise. Lucas could not prevent his mind from running wild with analytics and observations. Unfortunately, Lucas had one very great weakness when it came to playing his djembe. Never could he think too much, else his left hemispheric operations would begin to overpower and stifle the right hemispheric ones critical to his performance. Before he could check himself, his mind crossed that most inopportune threshold.

This time, immediate recovery was impossible. No, the beat went completely awry, and Lucas, try as he might, could not play it off. He stopped and as he retreated within himself, internal silence rung absolute. Alexander, himself, stumbled to a halt. The worst Lucas could imagine just happened. Lucas looked petrified. Suddenly, the many eyes penetrating his soul overwhelmed him. He closed his eyes and let out a mental scream.

Alexander noticed Lucas' turmoil and gestured to the crowd for support. Never would this community give up on one of its own. They were a family of artists, and they had nothing but love to give. The crowd started to chant "you can do it! You can do it! You can do it!"

Lucas, roused by the cadence, opened his eyes to bear witness to this unreal reality. His eyes swept over the audience and then locked with Alexander's. Alexander grinned and nodded. Lucas smiled and inhaled deeply. He began a slow, steady pounding sending resonating bass into the universe. He was no longer only his person, his body. At this moment, he was one with every single member of the audience, humanity, and all of existence. Here was a moment when the universe flowed with love. Lucas continued his steady pounding until he felt his coffer overflowing with love, then transitioned back into the rhythm of the song.

Right on cue, Alexander chimed in, and once again, the grand finale began. This time, Lucas was sure to make no mistake. The intensity slowly increased throughout, and as the ending neared, Lucas ventured to attempt the solo of his life. Alexander strummed in a broken beat to accent Lucas as he banged away in any and every musical direction. The crowd yelled their approval, and Lucas brought the beat back to that steady boom, boom, boom. Slowly the drum faded out, and the song finished. Applause sounded from the audience along with shouts and whistles. They had done it. They made a dream come true.

They hung around the bar to enjoy a few more performances, but the time arrived when they knew they must be off. Lucas bade his father farewell and thanked him for his support. Then, Alexander and Lucas exited the bar and walked toward Alexander's home.

"That was awesome!" Lucas bellowed. "I've never had so much fun playing my djembe before, and the support we got from the crowd, I didn't know that was possible."

"Yeah man, that's the universe taking care of itself. When we need it most, the universe is there to give us the love and support we need."

"It has never done that for me before. At least, not like that." Lucas looked wide eyed into the distance. "That was powerful, much more powerful than ever before."

"Maybe, you just weren't as in tune to the universe and the moment it existed in as you are now. Maybe, you are becoming aware of the absoluteness of its existence."

A smile spread across Lucas' face as he strode harder and quicker barely holding back his urge to skip. Lucas felt as though the entire universe embraced him with such love never known to him. All his fears and worries dissipated simply with an ethereal embrace. Desperately, he clung to the tranquility he knew would soon leave him, for all good things, in his experience, never last or never truly existed.

Suddenly, it dawned on him that in order to maintain this internal bliss he must manifest it in the external world. On the peak of this epiphany, Lucas jumped into a skip while howling as loudly as he could. The force of his backpack colliding with his lower back only served to propel him further. Alexander chimed in his own passionate howl, but he left the skipping to Lucas.

The bars and other buildings passed without trace, nor did the passersby catch Lucas' attention. He only saw the road before him and that amorphous abstraction of his destination. So caught up in where he was going, he forgot to take note of the journey. This tunnel vision could not last long, however, the universe allowed him this moment of blind anticipation before it reminded him of his purpose.

They reached the parking lot, and Alexander began his winding path once more. This time, Lucas let go of his logical compulsions and followed Alexander's suit, weaving back and forth between cars and letting his feet land wherever they like. When they neared the first fence, Lucas moved to climb it, but Alexander stopped him.

"We are going to enter this way." Alexander pointed to a section further to the left.

"Why climb over there?" Lucas asked but soon discovered that climbing was not what Alexander had in mind.

Alexander lifted the section slightly and pulled it toward him. The section swung open revealing a much more direct route to his home. He stuck out his arm gesturing his welcoming of Lucas.

"Why didn't we go this way before?" Lucas asked incredulously, a little divided on how he should feel.

"I only take those I know this way. Last time, we just met, so I didn't show you this way."

For a moment, Lucas mulled over the situation and concluded any disdain would be from a naïve understanding and quickly shook any negative emotions away. "That's smart. You have to be careful," he finally replied.

"Yup." Alexander returned the fence to its proper position and walked to the section they would have to climb. Alexander decided to climb first without his gear. Once he made it to the other side, Lucas handed Alexander their things one at a time. After they passed over the gear, Lucas climbed the fence and joined Alexander on the other side.

They would also use a different method to scale the twenty foot wall on which Alexander's home resided. Alexander went up the normal way first leaving Lucas and their equipment behind except for a long, thick, and sturdy rope. At the top, Alexander securely tied one end of the rope to a column and threw the other end down to Lucas. "You can carry the equipment as you use the rope to walk up the wall."

"That looks awesome!" Lucas' eyes gleamed with joy. "But, I'll have to make multiple trips."

Lucas threw on his backpack, and then, put Alexander's on across his chest. He grabbed the rope and began pulling himself. To climb, Lucas leaned forward as he grasped higher up the rope, then held tightly as he walked one foot up at a time. He repeated this process until he reached the top, but along the way he could not resist the thrill of looking down and watching the distance between him and the ground grow more and more.

Lucas dropped the backpacks off at the top and descended using the rope to start the process over again. He put Alexander's guitar on his back with its strap clinging to his chest and hung his djembe by its makeshift rope strap from his shoulder.

"You sure you can carry both of those?" Alexander asked more concerned for the instruments than Lucas.

"Yeah, I got it. Don't worry."

Lucas confidently took the rope in his hands and began his struggle upwards, however, he made the struggle look deceitfully easy until about halfway up when the djembe slipped off his shoulder. Lucas grunted as his balance shifted precariously, and he raised his arm to stop the djembe from smashing into the concrete wall. The attempt, somewhat successful, managed to lessen the blow but not prevent it. "Damn!" Lucas snarled.

"It's all good man. You got it."

Lucas adjusted the djembe back to his shoulder and started climbing again. No other mishap occurred to both's relief, but getting over the top of the wall now served as a challenge. Alexander tried to help by unburdening Lucas of his djembe, but Lucas was determined to finish on his own. He leaned forward pressing against his djembe as his djembe pressed lightly against the edge of the wall and grabbed further up the rope, so he could better pull himself up. With one great heave he gained enough elevation to place his foot on the edge and almost falling, stepped onto the level surface of Alexander's home. He made it, but barely.

"Great job, man!" Alexander encouraged as he help Lucas remove the instruments.

"That's it right? I don't want to do that anymore."

"Yeah, that's everything."

Alexander led Lucas to the corner where he slept and wanted to place their gear. "This is where I sleep. Let's go ahead and set up our pallets."

Alexander laid down his bag and began untying the twine holding his rolled bedding, and Lucas did likewise. First, Alexander placed his sheet down to help prevent his blankets from getting dirty. As he unfolded his queen size blanket, Lucas placed his sheet on top of Alexander's. Alexander looked confused and began to speak but remained silent.

"Oh, is this okay," Lucas asked seeing Alexander's reaction, "or do I need to make my own pallet?"

Only the most miniscule twitch of a corner of Alexander's mouth hinted at the smoothness by which he held an indifferent countenance. "Well, we will have more cushion if we put our blankets together. It will be more comfortable."

Lucas took this as affirmation and continued to adjust the sheet. Next, Alexander spread his queen size blanket atop the sheets, and again, Lucas did the same. On top of this, they would lay, so they placed their pillows on their respective halves and laid out the twin size blankets that would serve as their covers. Then, Alexander grabbed his bat and placed it under the first queen size blanket at the edge of where he would sleep. Lucas did the same with his wooden pole.

After they adjusted everything to their satisfaction, both sat against the sloping wall at the head of their pallet using their pillows to support their backs. Above them danced silvery shadows of incorporeal creatures skimming the tops of tiny waves rippling across the bayou. Lucas lost himself in that majestic display enamored by the simplicity of its creation. Simple because no effort beyond that of existence itself was needed. His thoughts trailed eventually to a point that never occurred to him. Surely, he thought, all things in existence emanate such exuberant beauty, but why he hadn't noticed this, now obvious, before eluded him. What is more, he did not understand why, even with this new understanding, he still could not fully appreciate the exuberance surrounding him.

Alexander stirred pulling Lucas away from his contemplation to a new stimulus. He watched as Alexander rose and walked to a pile of things already present when they arrived.

"I just realized I have a towel over here we can put under the instruments." He rummaged through what Lucas would normally consider grotesque junk and pulled out a red towel spotted with dirt and leaves.

"That's better than the sand and concrete for sure. Good idea." Lucas' appreciation was, to him, oddly genuine. Already, he was beginning to reconstruct his schema for luxury.

Lucas rose and walked over to the instruments. He held them while Alexander laid out the towel, then placed them down again. Both sat back down, and Lucas removed his shoes. His feet rejoiced at the touch of fresh air with wiggling toes and stretching ankles. Alexander's feet also craved such pleasure, so he, too, took off his shoes.

Lucas filled the auditory void with "Today was a pretty good day. A great start for our journey."

"Definitely. That was my first time playing on stage sober. I played *a lot* better this time." Alexander chuckled a little then continued. "But yeah, I can't think of anything better. It's perfect the way it is. A good start usually indicates a great finish."

"I felt whole, complete when we played especially after I messed up and everyone encouraged us to continue. That moment showed me something never revealed to me, something within me, something good, great even. I will never forget that moment. It's as if a missing piece of my being was simply handed to me after all these years of intensive searching."

"It's the good vibes of the universe that made you feel that way. Everyone there was there to give love and support."

"Maybe, that's what I am missing. Maybe, that's the key to unlocking my full potential of existence, to expressing myself fully."

"Absolutely! That's everyone's key. We can't be ourselves without love, and unfortunately, our society conditions us to not love ourselves or others. There's so much hate towards people who are different, who don't look a certain way or act a certain way, and people who are struggling to protect themselves from hate by hating. There's so much judgment there's no wonder why so many are depressed and anxious. It's impossible to be happy and at peace if you live with this conditioning. Too many bad vibes."

"You're right! I hardly see any acts of love. Not at home, school, or in general society. How can something so important be so scarce?"

"That is definitely a great mystery. I haven't figured that out yet."

"Something so fundamental couldn't simply disappear. That just doesn't make sense. Either we started without love and have developed this far, or we had love in the beginning but was, somehow, taken from us. Either way, the situation is dire, very dire indeed. What I just learned from my experience tonight is that in order for humanity and perhaps, everything else in existence to fulfill completely their potentialities we need love in abundance and without conditions, because love is a deep appreciation and acceptance of people and things for who or what they are. It's appreciating them for the beauty of their existence in itself without requiring alterations. Without this we will forever feel inadequate and hate ourselves and others and all of existence. So many people don't realize the world they are creating!"

"Yeah, man. We have complete control over the love we have. People just don't chose to do much with it."

"Exactly! Love is like a resource, a fuel. We use it to live and create, and the irony is we use love to foster hate! That has to be the pinnacle of tragedy."

"You have a point there, man. What I find most interesting is how humanity still searches for salvation, but we already found it. It's love, but for some reason, many are afraid of it. They act as though loving all of existence will lead to disaster. They avoid it as though it were some type of apocalyptic force, and that's why we don't progress and achieve our salvation on Earth."

"Well, now, that may be they true pinnacle of tragedy: to believe what will save us will destroy us. What a trap to be stuck in! That, there, is the best example of the mud we must rise from."

"We've got a lot of work to do if we are to overcome that. A lot of growth and a lot of time. It's definitely the biggest challenge humanity faces, right now."

"Yeah, but we will overcome this. We will rise from the mud. I feel it. The evolutionary currents of the universe direct us towards that goal. It's our destiny to evolve, to fulfill our potentialities to realize further potentialities. I have faith we will. I have to believe."

"Me too, man. I couldn't keep on living without believing that."

"Let's do something about it! We have everything we need: our minds, our hearts, and our bodies."

Yeah man, we will, for sure, but it's late, and I need some sleep. We'll figure something out tomorrow. After all, it's a new dawn, and we will be refreshed."

"Yeah, alright. I'm tired too."

Both slid down to lay on the pallet covering themselves with their blankets and repositioning their pillows. Alexander found a comfortable position almost immediately, while Lucas tossed and turned learning how his body preferred to interact with the hard surface. Once satisfied, Lucas closed his eyes and attempted to drift to sleep.

Only a moment later, Lucas said "Tomorrow will be another great day."

"Yes, it will be," Alexander mumbled. "Good night."

"Night." This time, Lucas fell asleep instantly.

As they slept, the silvery lights danced above them in that endless cycle of motion. From afar, the lights appeared to encapsulate them in aura of beauty as though they slept in a cocoon to awake metamorphosed into something different, something more beautiful. All would become clear in the morning.

DAY ONE

Lucas opened his eyes slowly revealing a blur of light. He blinked and wiped the sleep from his eyes. A sharp pang ran down his side. He writhed slightly trying to quickly counteract whatever was causing the pain. When he sat up, more of his body cried out to him pleading for his attention and care. The concrete bed proved more troublesome than anticipated.

Lucas rose from the pallet and took account of his surroundings. Alexander still slept seemingly unperturbed by the hardness of the concrete. The sun shone brightly leaving nothing unilluminated, and the water gleamed as it flowed with the tilt of the Earth and the pull of gravity. The wind, too, was awake and blowing strongly, swaying trees, ruffling the grass, and caressing anyone within its reach. The trees breathed deeply while the squirrels scurried hither and thither, and the birds rotated from perch to perch.

Lucas inhaled the fresh air brought by the wind and stretched those parts still pulsating with pain. Feeling the urge to relieve his bladder, Lucas searched for what would serve as the restroom. He decided, sleepily, that the ledge facing the park below would have to do. He walked to the ledge not thinking of the inappropriate nature of what he was about to do, so he did not bother to consider any unwanted eyes. As he urinated off the ledge, he caught sight of a horse far in the distance. The horse moved from behind a tree, and Lucas could see the police officer riding it and his partner following on another horse.

Suddenly, the context of where he was and what he was doing returned, and he quickly finished and retreated to the cover provided by the columns a bit startled by his recklessness. After he calmed down, he took another gander at the horses and realized many people rushed about the parking lot. Many of which had the unmistakable appearance of college students. There were even people crossing the bridge he was under. So much activity, he wondered how he did not notice.

Lucas returned to the pallet and sat against the slopping wall. He watched the ripples running through the water, the trees swaying, and the animals darting back and forth. He remained peacefully observing for some time, however time was of no importance to him. Lucas felt at home here, more at home here than at his dad's house, without any worries or concerns. True, there were still responsibilities to his person, but something seemed significantly different. He felt free, but free from what?

I'm really doing this. The strangest thing about it is that it feels so natural, so right, but am I not supposed to be encountering some sort of disastrous event, something that will tear me to pieces? I suppose it's still early on.

Alexander rolled over. Lucas glanced over to see if he had woken, but Alexander still slept. He returned to his meditations.

What am I getting from all this? Why am I doing this? Even though I don't have the answers to these questions, I feel like this is exactly what I am supposed to do. Anyone else would think I'm doing something stupid. I'm sure my dad thinks so, but that doesn't matter. This is what I have to do.

Alexander rolled over again, but this time woke with a grunting moan.

Lucas greeted him back to the conscious world "Good morning."

Alexander rubbed his eyes and ran his hand through his hair. "Morning," he mumbled.

Looking for affirmation of what he already concluded, Lucas said "I saw some cops on horses. I was standing right in the open. I should try not to be seen, huh?"

Alexander, still waking, sat up and said plainly "Yeah, that would be a good idea." Then, Alexander stood and walked to the same ledge Lucas had urinated off of and relieved himself.

Lucas began to warn Alexander about the cops being on that side, but when he looked over he found no trace of them. Seeing no point in lingering, Lucas reverted his attention back to his needs and decided to brush his teeth. He retrieved his toothbrush and paste from his bag and grabbed his water bottle. He walked up the sloping wall he sat against earlier until he was nearly to the top. He wet his toothbrush, applied paste, and began brushing.

As he brushed his teeth, he looked at the buildings on the opposite side of the bayou. The largest building had thick metal bars on every window, and the building itself was surrounded by a large fence. He realized the building must be a prison located just outside the downtown area. Suddenly, the feeling of freedom intensified. He rinsed his mouth out and rinsed off his toothbrush, then went to join

Alexander on the pallet.

"So what's the plan for today?" Lucas asked.

"We pack up, then go see what the city has in store for us. If you're hungry, we can try to play for money or food."

Lucas had not thought of food yet, but now, the topic started his gastric processes making his stomach rumble and feel like a burning pit begging to be filled. "That sounds perfect!"

After lazing around a bit longer, they began packing up their things. First, they rolled up their bedding and tied the bundles to prevent them from unraveling. They collected whatever they removed from their bags and returned them. Once they collected everything, they tied their rolls to their bags in such a way that the bundle would rest as much as possible on the upper portion of their bags to be supported primarily by their shoulders. This provided the proper weight distribution that would spare them much unnecessary discomfort.

Alexander threw down the large rope they would use to scale down as Lucas put on his backpack and picked up his djembe. While Alexander gathered his things, Lucas began his dissent. He held the rope firmly with both hands and leaned backwards over the ledge. The first step was the hardest because he had to step the two feet drop to reach the sloping part of the wall. Once there, the rest of the way was easy. Simply, one step after another while alternating grips. He liked this method much more than climbing without a rope.

With a thud Lucas landed on the ground and then stepped back to watch Alexander. As he watched, Lucas reflected on how absurd the act appeared through his frame of reference. He associated climbing like this, especially with their equipment, with rock climbing somewhere in the wilderness far from civilization, but here they were, in the very heart of one of the largest metropolitan areas in the United States.

When Alexander reached the bottom, he laid down his guitar and removed his backpack, so he could throw the rope back to the top. Satisfied that the rope was out of sight, Alexander picked his things back up and led the way to the exit. They passed their bags over the top, vaulted the fence, and exited through the sliding section.

The crunch of the grass beneath their feet brought a sense of joy to the both of them. Something about the way in which a living entity supported another, one piece of existence stacked upon another, giving rise to yet another interconnectedness: the atmosphere on top of and imbibing the biosphere which in turn leads still to a greater whole with each piece fulfilling its role. The flow of purpose and of existence swelled within the two a great eagerness.

A sudden realization struck Alexander. "I just thought of a great place for us to play. There's this little strip of food joints near a medical center. I'm sure we'll get food there."

"Sounds good. How far is it?"

"Not too far, but we have to get on the train."

Conveniently, a train station was just across the street. As they made their way to the platform, a train passed, so they would have to wait for the next. Alexander laid down his baggage and sat down on one of the metal benches. Lucas sat beside him.

"So, do you always ride the train without paying?" asked Lucas.

Shamelessly Alexander replied "Yeah, man. I haven't been caught yet, but it's ridiculous how they try to control and regulate transportation. Besides, the train should be a free service to the people of this city."

"But, it is not free. Don't you think it's unethical to ride without paying?"

"Well, it depends on how you look at it. If you only see a law and me breaking the law, then I suppose it is, but that's not how I see it. I have no money, and I need to get across town. Add my nerve damage, and I don't care about the fee. I just want to go from point A to point B with the least amount of pain as possible."

"When you put it that way, I'm inclined to ignore the fee as well. I guess it's not as simple as I thought."

"Yeah, and that's why I think unconditional laws like that are ridiculous. It's just someone trying to make themselves feel better by controlling others. I don't pay attention to that nonsense."

"I never thought of it that way."

The next train arrived, stopped, and opened its doors. They readied themselves to board, and as Lucas walked to the entrance he noticed a digital sign flashing. To his relief, the sign stated that all train rides were free to everyone until the end of the month. He hurried to catch up to Alexander, and they seated themselves.

Not much was exchanged between the two for the duration of their ride, but everywhere bustled with activity. People dashed madly down the sidewalks desperate to achieve. The cars rushing to unknown finish lines. The people on the train talked to one another, talked on their phones, listened to music, or just sat silently staring out the windows. None of this, however, interested Lucas. His attention focused inward on what churned within.

The train jerked to a stop, and Alexander said "This is it."

They exited and crossed the street to the strip of restaurants Alexander spoke of. At the other end of the block, a man was already hard at work playing the trombone, but Alexander showed no concern. In fact, he chose the middle of the block to set up giving the man some space while allowing for competition.

Lucas, however, could not help concerning himself with the effect of their proximity on the man. "Shouldn't we give him more space? Won't we be intruding?"

"No, we're good. He's at the best spot. Most of the foot traffic is over there, and I want to get as close as possible."

"But, won't we be getting in the way of his making money?"

"Maybe, but if we don't, we have to find another place. I don't feel like going anywhere else. Besides, we are already here, and I'm hungry."

"But what if he's hungry too?"

"We have to think about our own survival first before we can go about thinking of others."

Lucas disagreed with this reasoning, but he held his tongue. He was here to learn, and if this was how Alexander did things, he would acquiesce. Lucas decided it was best to use this experience as fodder for growth, though he had no idea what growth. He laid down his things and positioned himself to play.

Alexander began playing one of the songs performed the night before, and shortly, Lucas filled in the rhythm playing as though he were back on stage but strove to play even better. People passed with either indifference or minor expressions of curiosity. Some even seemed quite annoyed that two young men and another man awkwardly spaced apart would have the audacity to pollute their routine reprieve with unattractive spectacles and discordant noise.

After the first song ended, Alexander stood up and walked toward a Styrofoam cup on the ground beside a trashcan. Satisfied, he returned and placed the cup at the front of their set up. "We need something to collect money in."

They started up again, and they played all the songs they knew, which were not many, until a sympathetic ear bent down and placed a dollar bill into the cup.

"Thank you so much!" Alexander sang in time with the music.

Lucas gave his thanks by nodding and accenting with a rapid succession of staggered beats concluded with a rolling transition back to the rhythmic skeleton.

The sympathetic ear grew a glowing smile, then turned to walk away. Lucas was beginning to lose hope, but this gift revitalized him. His playing, too, regained life, and he pushed on. Alexander chose the songs and their order, and once he cycled through them a second time, he decided it was time to improvise. Lucas, of course, did not mind the sudden shift, because he could play to almost anything. Alexander chose a Blues melody and gave Lucas a chance to settle into the rhythm before he began singing.

Abruptly and loudly, Alexander started singing "We are so hungry! We haven't eaten since yesterday. Please, spare some change so we can sooth our aching bellies. If we don't eat today, I'm afraid we'll lose all hope and fade to dust as we finally given in. Spare some change. We only want to eat. You can even buy me a sandwich. Subway is just over there. A six inch sub sounds amazing right now!"

A man looked at them as he passed, and Alexander took advantage of this connection. "You, sir! Help! Feed the hungry, please. I swear it's not a gimmick. We just want a sandwich." The man could not prevent himself from smiling for being signaled out. Moved as he was by Alexander's enthusiasm, he dropped five one dollar bills in the cup.

This very generous offering could never go without Alexander's blessing, so with a new vigor he bellowed "Oh, thank you, thank you, thank you! Sandwich get ready; here I come!" The man left still smiling, and Alexander's outburst drew even more attention to them. A woman walked over and stood in front of them listening closely. Alexander continued improvising using his hunger as his muse, and Lucas even contributed a "We are so hungry!" every now and then. Eventually, Alexander needed to stop and rest, however, Lucas could have kept going. He was having so much fun.

The woman, still standing in front of them asked "So, are you guys trying to be musicians?"

"Well mam, we are musicians," Alexander replied, "but right now we are just trying to get some food. I'm also a traveler, and this is how I provide for myself on my travels."

"Oh, I see. What about you?" She gestured to Lucas.

"Me, I'm on a quest for knowledge, though I'm not sure what I'm looking for. I met my friend here last month, and I'm spending time with him on the streets for a bit."

She allowed herself a moment to digest what they told her, then responded. "Interesting. Well keep it up. I wish the best for you." Before she walked away, she placed a five dollar bill in their cup, and they thanked her.

"Sweet! We almost have enough for two sandwiches." Lucas exclaimed. "We're just a couple of dollars short."

Alexander began playing again, and Lucas quickly followed. They cycled through another round of their songs, but no one else offered any more money. Lucas felt frustrated at how close they were to eating yet so far. He decided he wanted to take a more direct approach to obtaining the funds.

"Can I just ask people for money?" Lucas asked Alexander.

"Sure, why not? Give it a shot."

Lucas rose eagerly and walked to a table of women about twenty feet away. As he neared, he timidly addressed the first person to make eye contact. "Excuse me. My friend and I," he pointed to Alexander, "are trying to get some Subway, but we're a couple dollars short. Could you help us out?"

The woman he asked looked stoically at him and said "No, sorry."

Lucas made eye contact with the rest of the party and asked "can any of you help?"

All of them either silently shook their heads or said "no, sorry."

Lucas felt defeated as though he failed in some way more significant than merely acquiring funds. "Well, thanks anyway," he said awkwardly and clumsily moved away.

He spotted a man in a white doctor's coat walking down the sidewalk in his direction and hurriedly approached him. "Excuse me, sir. I'm trying to get some Subway, but I'm a couple dollars…"

The man cut Lucas off "I don't have any money" and kept on walking.

Lucas kept searching and approached another to be met with a similar answer. He tried a few more times to no avail, then decided to sit back down with Alexander. He sloped his shoulders as he sat, defeat emanating from him. He knew better, but he could not stop his foolishness. Certainly, most would meet the same fate as he did, but this was *Lucas*. He was used to getting his way. Someone was always there to help him in one way or another. Although he never asked for money from strangers before, he felt if anyone was to have success, it would be him.

"You need to ask more assertively like you would ask your dad for something," Alexander coached. "Ask like the answer is already yes."

Lucas recoiled in disgust, "But, that's ridiculous. How can I act entitled like that?"

"Well, you are entitled. You are a human being, and as a human being your needs should be met by the society. After all, that's the point of society."

"Maybe, but I can't just be entitled without doing anything. I have to work or contribute something."

"Of course, you do, and you are. How many of these people talk or even think about all the things you've been talking about? Not many. That's worth something more than some stupid job. You should have your needs met, because it's people like you who are going to keep this world from destroying itself. You simply existing is doing plenty. All of these people should want to help you, and all you want to do is help people. Any help they give you will be returned, so there is nothing wrong with you asking for help. If anything, it's the best thing for all of us."

Stunned, Lucas looked up but could not bring himself to make eye contact with Alexander. Instead, he stared at the glass door across from them. He desperately wanted to absorb everything Alexander just told him, but again, something prevented him from accepting the message within his core. Lucas muddled over the idea that simply existing made him worthy of support in his most peripheral cognizance. Every cell in his body screamed in terror of this notion, but the reason eluded him.

Alexander continued "Anyone doing what you are doing should be taken care of. Ideally, we all would appreciate everyone and support each other but especially people like you. You're not asking for money for alcohol or drugs. You're asking for food so you can continue this journey, and so you can learn whatever is out here for you to learn."

Now was not the time for him to truly absorb this message Lucas concluded, if any such time existed, rather now was the time to put faith in himself and to believe in the good he was doing by putting himself in this situation. Asking for money suddenly became imperative for his development. Something was out here for him to learn, and this was a part of it.

"Okay," Lucas said as he stood. He would try again, and this time it would be successful. He walked to the side opposite of where he first tried. The foot traffic being heavy, he immediately found someone to ask.

More confidently he said "Hey man, my friend and I need to eat, but we're only a couple dollars short. Can you give us a couple bucks?"

Despite the much improved approach, the man said he did not have any cash. Lucas thanked the man and moved on to the next.

"Excuse me, my friend and I need to eat. Can you give us a couple of dollars?"

"No, sorry."

Lucas turned around and saw another man amongst a group of friends walking his way. This was the one.

"Excuse me, my friend and I need to eat, but we are a couple of dollars short." Lucas pulled the bundle of cash out of his pocket and held it for the man to see.

Lucas had approached the man while he was listening to his friend, so he did not fully hear Lucas. Suspicious, he asked "What do you want?"

"I need a couple of bucks."

The man wrinkled his brow and pointed to the wad of cash. "You have money right there."

Lucas stood his ground and asserted "Yeah, I know, but I'm a couple of dollars short of buying my friend and me Subway." He pointed to Alexander to indicate who his friend was.

"Alright." The man said, and he pulled out his wallet and handed Lucas two dollars.

"Thanks a lot!" Lucas gave the man a big smile and then, walked back to Alexander.

Once he reached Alexander, He exclaimed "I did it! We can eat now!"

Alexander grinned. "Great job, man! I'm hungry. Let's eat."

They picked up their things and eagerly headed to Subway. As they waited in line, each figured out what they would order.

"I'm going to get a six inch meatball marinara." Lucas shared excitedly. "What are you going to get?"

"I'm a vegetarian, so I'll get a veggie sandwich."

This caught Lucas by surprise, and he shook his head in disbelief. "Now, how do you manage that on the streets?"

"Just like this."

"But isn't it harder to be a vegetarian? I mean, I know it can be more expensive, but I don't see how it can provide enough nutrition when you don't eat very often."

Alexander shrugged. "Well, I get by."

It was their turn to order, so Alexander moved closer to the lady impatiently awaiting to take their orders and placed his. After Alexander finished, Lucas told the lady what he wanted, excitedly pointing to the toppings he wanted, and they moved down to the cashier. Lucas pulled out the wad of cash and handed it to the cashier with a proud smile. The cashier, unimpressed, took the cash, counted it, and then broke the bad news.

Annoyed, she said "You are 31¢ short."

Lucas cried "Oh, man!" as he patted his pockets, feeling for change he knew was not there but hoped by a miracle it would appear. He looked to Alexander, who just shrugged. Then, he looked imploringly around the subway as the fear and frustration of coming so close to obtaining food only to fall so short engulfed him.

Suddenly, the man behind them in line stepped forward and handed the cashier the remaining charge. Lucas' eyes widened with joy, and he almost shouted "Thank you, sir! Thank you!" The man merely nodded and gestured not to worry.

Lucas turned to Alexander in excitement "Yes!"

Alexander smiled and casually retrieved his sandwich and cup from the cashier. Lucas did the same, and they went to the soda fountain to fill their cups. Alexander chose Coke while Lucas chose his favorite, Root Beer. After securing their lids and inserting their straws, they walked to a table directly adjacent to the large glass windows near the entrance and sat two seats over from a rather unpleasant looking character. They began unwrapping their sandwiches, and both took as big of a bite their mouths allowed. Lucas moaned with pleasure. It was early afternoon, and he had not eaten since the night before, much longer than he was used to going without eating.

After swallowing, Lucas exclaimed "This is so good! I can't believe this. I'm on the streets with no money, but here I am eating my favorite sandwich and drinking my favorite soda, and I have two cookies to boot. I really didn't expect this."

"Well, today is a good day. It's not always this good. Sometimes you have to eat worse or less or not at all, but we earned this meal. We should be proud."

Lucas expressed his agreement by taking another gigantic bite. Alexander was about to as well when the man sitting near them addressed him in mumbled and slurred speech.

"Heeyy, can ju hep me get some cigarettes? I got ze money. They jus won't let me buy 'em." As he spoke, drool slowly dripped from his bottom lip to his shirt. He did not seem to notice or care as he kept his mouth open wide while staring at Alexander with his glazed eyes.

Lucas could not understand a single word the man said and looked extremely uncomfortable, but Alexander, sitting slightly closer and more adept at understanding this particular form of speech, heard enough. He took on a compassionate disposition as he asked the man "You have money for a pack?"

"Yeah, thatz wat I say."

"Alright," Alexander said cautiously. "I'll help you. There's a store around the corner. Let's go."

He put down his sandwich, took a sip of soda, and rose from his seat. Alexander waited as the man stumbled off his seat and began wobbling to the door. The man's pants, immediately upon his standing, started falling down, but he held them up somewhat, at least in the front, with his hand. Each step brought the man's pants further down his rear revealing his feces stained underwear. Alexander opened the door for the man and realized the unfortunate unfolding of events but still maintained the will to help.

Lucas watched as they crossed in front of him and walked out of sight down the sidewalk. Despite the grotesque display, Lucas's hunger goaded him back to eating his sandwich with an uncomfortable rumbling of his stomach. He managed to finish three fourths of his sandwich before Alexander reappeared. As Alexander sat back down, Lucas remarked "That didn't take very long."

Alexander looked a little flustered. "That's because I had to leave the guy. His pants almost fell down completely, his junk was hanging out, and he kept harassing people along the way for cigarettes. I had to get away from him. He was causing way too much trouble."

"Oh, sorry you had to deal with that." Lucas said uncertain how to respond to such a phenomenon.

"Yeah, it's all good. I wanted to help him, but he made it way too difficult. That's the kind of person that gives homeless people a bad image. I don't know why he's out here. He needs help, but I'm not surprised that people would just let him suffer like this." Alexander sighed and continued eating his sandwich.

"That's horrible! This is exactly what infuriates me about civilization. We create people that we deem ugly or unfit, and then we either destroy them or leave them to destroy themselves. This is nothing new. The Spartans, for example, would inspect their newly born, and any considered unfit were killed or left to die so not to contaminate the population with inferior genes. They wanted only the 'fittest' to live. Nowadays, since our moralities have changed to condemn such behavior, we can't kill the unfit. Instead, we treat them like the way this guy is treated.

"We say it's Social Darwinism and thus natural, but we are the ones who decide what is 'fit' by how we design the structure of civilization. Fitness, in the human world, is an arbitrary manifestation of the most influential people's values. It is absolutely not an objective or natural fact. We don't live in nature like we used to. True, human civilization is itself a part of nature, but it's a secondary nature *we* created on top of primary nature or first nature. We have total control over how it exists.

"We don't treat people this way because we believe in Social Darwinism. We treat them this way because we are in denial. If we accept responsibility for the existence of these 'unfit' people, then we will have to acknowledge our own faults and fallibilities. We would have to acknowledge that we are responsible for creating the atrocious circumstances and great sufferings that made these 'unfit' unfit. These people weren't born unfit. We made them so by declaring that they are flawed rather than the structure of civilization. Yes, even those born with physical and mental disorders are no longer necessarily unfit. We have advanced technologically enough that such hindrances to life no longer impede existence as ultimately as in ages past. Now, it is our neglect of our own people that creates the 'unfit'.

"I would help people like that if I knew how and if I had the resources to do so, but I'm powerless. I think that's the hardest thing to bear."

Alexander chomped down on the last piece of his sandwich. After taking a sip of soda to wash the last bit of masticated sandwich, he commented "Hey man, you make a great point there, but you're not powerless! If you can see it and describe it, you can do something about it. Like you said last night, we have everything we need."

"But what will awaken people on a mass scale? That's what we will need to truly overhaul the current paradigm. Only a collective effort will accomplish reformation on a civilizational scale."

"Well, we might not have a way of doing that, but we can reach individuals. We can change the world one person at a time, man, and that's something meaningful."

"Perhaps, it's a place to start." Lucas rested his chin on his palm as he stared off into space.

Alexander began to realize the wavering of Lucas' confidence and hope, the undulation from moment to moment. He realized Lucas had yet to fully ground himself in himself, and he, now, sought to help in the most significant way one could help another: Alexander was going to show Lucas the foundation he has been desperately seeking is within himself, that the only solid ground in this abyssal existence resides deep within his own cognizance. He would show him, but first, the time must be made. For now, he would coax Lucas to make his own fertile experiences to grow from.

"We can write a poem or a song and perform it on the streets."

Slowly, Lucas looked from his thoughts to Alexander. "Yeah, we could do that." Alexander remained silent as he allowed Lucas' gears to turn and smiled as Lucas' eyes brightened. "Yes, we can do that! That will work. No one would expect anything like that. Two homeless looking young men reciting poetry out of the blue that actually stirs something within them. It's better than I thought. There's so much power in it. We have to do it."

"Sounds like a plan." Alexander collected the wrappings and other trash from his meal and stood to throw them away.

Lucas rose to do the same, and at the trashcan, he asked "But, what do we write about? I can feel it, but I still can't quite make it out."

Alexander walked back to their things and picked up his backpack.

"Let's think about it on the train. I don't like the vibes here. We need the right vibes if we are going to accomplish this."

Uncertain he understood exactly what Alexander meant but reflecting on the unfavorable attitudes of the majority in the area, Lucas consented and prepared to leave. They exited the Subway and walked directly to the platform in the middle of the street. A minute later, a train arrived, and they boarded.

The thrust of embarkment firmly forced Lucas against his seat where he stayed tilting his head back and closed his eyes. He listened to the sounds of the train, the humming of muffled grinding of wheels on tracks. He felt the vibrations and the shaking of cars. Somehow, he thought, he could convert the kinetic energy driving the train into the energy of thought by merely focusing on it and willing it to course through him, but his attempts were in vain. Giving up such mystical thinking, he opened his eyes and sat upright.

"We need to figure out what to say," stated Lucas. "First of all, we need to figure out what is available to us, like what our circumstances really mean and how we feel. Why we are both out here already has a great deal of material."

"Well," Alexander replied "I chose to be out here at first because it was better than living at home, but now, I prefer it because I feel alive out here. Every day is precious. I feel like when I'm out here, I'm truly in tune with the universe. I feel like I'm surviving, like I'm earning my life. For some reason, I hate being in buildings. They make me feel trapped and depressed."

"And, I'm out here because something vital is missing in me, and I can't find it in society. Not to mention, I feel ostracized by the general populous. I don't fit in, but it's more than just my personality. My very perception of reality seems to differ irreconcilably with everyone else's. People appear happy with the way things are, but I find everything extremely flawed and often heinous."

"Yeah man, me too. Maybe, that's what we should focus on."

"Maybe. We need something that communicates what we both said, something that shows why we feel people in society aren't living and how it's their perceptions that need to change."

"That's exactly what we've been talking about all along. I'm sure we will be able to come up with something."

"Perhaps, but I wish I could drink coffee while I write. Coffee always helps me think better. Is there an IHOP around? We can get unlimited coffee for about three dollars each."

"Not in this area, but I know where one is. We have to take the bus to get there."

"Alright, I'm fine with that, but now, we need to get money for coffee."

The train came to a halt, and Alexander stood abruptly, grabbed his things, and said "Here's a great spot to make money," as he headed for the door. Lucas hurried to keep up but thought nothing of the acute shift in plans. This was becoming a normal, even expected mode of existence.

They stepped onto the platform and assessed their prospects. They were back on the side of downtown where Alexander's home resided and where Alexander spent most of his time. It was early evening when, for most, the work day came to an end. Already, traffic began congesting, and the sidewalks filled with pedestrians.

"I think it will be easier to hit up the bars around here later tonight. A lot of these people just got off work, and the last thing they want is to be bugged with the likes of us. We're not going to get anything right now, but later, we definitely will."

They decided to explore as they waited for that more opportune hour of generosity when the conditions were just right for the birth of benevolence. Lucas observed the people brushing past him in both directions, how they moved so economically with the least bit of inefficiency, how they focused as if wearing blinders, how they looked so tired, so worn. He would normally walk among them in similar fashion, but as of now, he found them bizarre in their behaviors, almost alien.

Lucas no longer walked with calculated precision. He no longer stared as though through a dark tunnel to the light of some distant exit. He no longer felt his limbs too heavy, nor his mind too sluggish. Lucas felt fluid, light, and free flowing. He did not focus on any one thing but all things surrounding him. He had become completely permeable to the existences around him.

Lucas returned to verbally processing the world with Alexander. "What do all these people value? Why are they here almost all week every week? What are they giving their existence to?"

"Well, they're here because their jobs are here, and they work so they can eat, support families, and fund their dreams. That's at the core of what they value."

"But, that doesn't make sense. It seems like a complete waste of time and potential. Having to work jobs, I mean. If the point of having jobs is to accomplish these core values, why not simply provide the means for those values without requiring 'work'? If we did that, wouldn't people have more time to fulfill greater potentials? We wouldn't have to worry about anything other than bringing our dreams to fruition and achieving our fullest potential."

"Yeah man, I agree, but the argument against that is society would collapse. People are afraid that other people won't do what's necessary to keep society going because they will be lazy and only take advantage of those benefits."

"So, it seems, to insure that people contribute in the ways someone or a specific group of people desire, the necessity for jobs was created and so were economic systems and social hierarchies. After all, some person or group of people had to decide what was important for civilization and thus what our values would be."

"Right, and because people perceive the world differently, these systems were created to persuade people to conform."

"That's a very nice way of describing slavery! That's exactly what our economies and social hierarchies represent. If we look closely, we'll find that our freedom is surely limited and mostly an illusion. We can choose our jobs, how we live, and there's social mobility, but it all is confined in a box or a mold. We have the freedom to choose from a pool of choices already chosen for us. It's slavery under the guise of liberty!"

"Whoa, man! I didn't think of it like that." Alexander allowed this notion to sink in. "You're right. You're actually right. We've been duped into believing we are free. That's why I'm out here, man, to break out of that slavery. I can't see any way of living in society without becoming a slave. That's why I plan on taking off to the woods to live away from this madness."

"And, that's why I am out here. I'm here to prove my hypothesis correct by observing civilization from the outside, so I can finally see the box I am trapped in."

A man smoking a cigarette walked toward them, and before he passed, Alexander asked him for one. The man, with only the slightest hint of inconvenience gave a cigarette and his lighter to Alexander. Once he lit the cigarette, Alexander returned the man's lighter and thanked him. Lucas waited patiently with his thoughts.

Then, they continued aimlessly walking down the sidewalk.

"That's it!" Lucas exclaimed. "We have to awaken everyone to their slavery by showing them the chains that bind them, and the most basic or fundamental of these chains are the distribution of resources and their regulation. I mean mainly food, water, and shelter which are distributed in proportion to individual wealth and regulated by corporations, the government, and other large entities. How much of these resources we receive is not determined by our need but by the amount of our contribution to prescribed facets of the current civilizational design, and they are seemingly regulated so that only a small group has control over their production and distribution, which inevitably gives this group great influence over us."

"Yeah, man." Alexander interjected. "I heard a corporation was genetically modifying crops to not produce seeds, so we have to buy more of their seeds. Or, like in the grocery store we see all these brands that are actually owned by a small number of large corporations."

"Exactly. Those are good examples of regulation, and they seem harmless until you try to live outside the box. Resources are plentiful to those who conform, but challenge the paradigm and you quickly meet a scarcity never imagined. That's what I'm learning out here."

"Yeah, you find that out immediately out here." There was a rueful poignancy to Alexander's statement. "You also find out the opposite. Those who conform more receive more. That only reinforces their conformity and gives them a sense of righteousness that conformity is right, and then, they have to look down on those who don't conform to protect their righteousness."

"Yes, good point. And, to help validate this vindictive precept, a social hierarchy was created. With a social hierarchy in place, it's much easier to feel justified in degrading others. Without one, there would be too much doubt for us to judge others as vehemently as we do now. Also, the social hierarchy creates a distraction for people to forget or never learn that all of this is arbitrary and created by us. As we climb the social ladder, we receive more resources and more of our psychological needs are met. Because we have been striving all our lives to obtain these, we again lose ourselves, but this time, in the euphoria, and we don't consider that it didn't have to be this way.

"So many distractions layered upon distractions! And, those who enjoy the upper tiers of the hierarchy without any concern for the paradigm remind me of those slaves, when slavery was more physically manifested, who treated other slaves poorly, so they could receive better treatment from their masters."

"Yeah, man! That's exactly it. I've been trying to put my finger on this. You just showed me much more clearly why I'm having such a hard time living in society."

"But, how do we wake people up to see this? The signs are all around them, yet they still don't seem to see. On second thought, we can't tell them their slaves, and we can't show them someone else controls their means to live. I think they know that in a way but do not appreciate the significance of it. Perhaps, the only way to reach them is to show them how the world could be if they woke up and took control of their existence."

"And, how do we do that? We can't just say things will be better. People are only willing to risk believing in this if they have solid proof, but how do we show what can only be dreamed?"

"Now, that is a great question, and perhaps, our greatest challenge." Lucas looked down as he walked, avoiding the cracks in the sidewalk. His brain churned and churned, but the answer to Alexander's question eluded him. He returned his gaze ahead. "We have reached quite the impasse. We can't show them a world other than our own, and pointing out what they already see won't be enough."

"If only dreams were enough, this would be so much easier."

"There's the answer! Dreams are enough. We just have to remind people that civilization is merely a manifestation of our dreams. We create the world around us, but our dreams are the blueprints. They are the only blueprints available to us. And, I don't mean only a select few dream and create. Everyone dreams up and creates civilization. I mean everyone. The civilization we have now exists because we all in one way or another, willingly or unwillingly at the very least abide by the dreams which make it and actively make those dreams a reality. All of this is built on and with dreams."

"Why didn't I think of that?" Alexander exclaimed. He raised up his arms and held them out indicating to the people around them as he asked "Why don't they think of that?"

"Because, they're too caught up in their own survival, and thinking this way only makes it harder to survive in the current paradigm. The structure strips people of their autonomy, and they stop thinking for themselves. It's too painful for them to maintain awareness of their slavery without knowing how to escape it. They are like animals in a cage trying to forget their confinement because they can't break or bend the bars. They are deluding themselves."

"Maybe, but with the knowledge of how dreams create civilization, we can finally break out. We can fight back and reclaim our autonomy!"

"That's what I hope. By obtaining an understanding of the mechanisms used to create civilization, we can create our own paradigm, our own civilizational structure, and then, the old design will dissipate in the presence of a more evolved one. But, we can't do this until we have a collective working together towards this evolution."

"Well, let's go make one! We'll wake people up. I know it." Alexander in his excitement concluded his sentiment with a loud, deep howl. Lucas welcomed this cathartic release and competed to out howl Alexander. Back and forth they went howling with a dire attempt to surpass the other.

The sun had gone down some time ago, and only the last remnants of the daily rush remained. The night life began to reveal itself as a new energy emanated from passersby, one of sensual desire. Alexander's sense for good vibes did not falter here. He chose a promising bar and led Lucas to a portion of the sidewalk slightly to its right. They laid their belongings down to serve as seats, and as Alexander situated himself, Lucas searched for a new container for collection. He chose a small cardboard box someone threw away after consuming the contents within.

Outside the bar, people stood smoking and drinking while discussing matters that caressed and soothed their racing minds. Others walked by pursuing the various stimuli available. Lucas noted how much of an ordeal their evaluations were. So much careful calculation to properly anesthetize the mind, to forget the world engulfing them. These were the people Lucas wanted to awaken, but still, he found himself incapable.

Alexander started strumming a familiar tune, and Lucas placed his longing aside to play his djembe. Immediately, they caught the attention of those not already intrigued by this unusual pair. Some stopped to listen. Others kept walking disregarding their presence. Despite the attention they received, no funds were procured, and after a while, they stopped to rest.

Lucas' stomach growled, and he quickly moved to rub it. "I'm hungry, man. All this walking makes you build up an appetite."

"Yeah man, it does. It's really hard when you can't get any food."

"Oh, I hope we get food!" As Lucas spoke, a man came into view and in his hand, a Styrofoam carton presumably filled with food. Lucas leaned over to Alexander and asked quietly "Can I ask that guy for his left overs?"

"Yeah, man. Go for it."

Lucas tried to stand, but his legs disobeyed his commands. "I can't do it."

"Yes, you can." Alexander encouraged.

Lucas stood but sat back down almost immediately. "I don't know why, but I can't." As the man passed directly in front of them, Lucas opened his mouth but could not speak.

Alexander waited to the last moment to step in. The man had gained a distance of twenty feet, but Alexander caught up and talked to the man, pointing at Lucas. Compassion radiated from the man's face as he quickly nodded and handed over his left overs. As Alexander headed back, Lucas' face brightened with joy, and he gestured in celebration.

"Yes!" Lucas exclaimed. "Thanks."

"Anytime, man." Alexander sat down and opened the carton. "Nachos, alright!"

Lucas and Alexander shared the meal as they sat observing the life around them. Alexander appreciated most Lucas' joy and enthusiasm toward the meal and praised himself for listening to his instincts. With every bite, Lucas expressed his happiness with positive exclamations and gratified moans. Moments like these undoubtedly reminded them both of the good born from their journey.

After they finished the sizable portion allotted them, they decided to resume playing and try again at earning money for coffee. They played for some time, but none of the many onlookers offered donations. Lucas began to lose hope and soon needed another break. Defeat crept upon him ready to devour all remaining life within him. Again, he was so close but so far from fulfilling his purpose.

Just before Lucas gave up entirely, the man who provided their evening meal reappeared. He carried a plastic bag bulging with spherical shapes. He approached the two young men and handed them the bag which they found filled with six oranges, four snack bars, two water bottles, and a package of beef jerky. To top it off, the man handed each a twenty dollar bill.

Lucas burst with gratitude yelling "Thank you! Thank you! Thank you!" and danced around with joy. The man and Alexander looked on with amusement, smiles wide across their faces. Alexander shook the man's hand and offered a praise of his own. Then, the man left them to their celebrations.

Lucas finally settled down enough to say "Now, we can get some coffee."

"Yeah, man. We just need to find the bus. It's getting late, so we better hurry before they stop for the night."

They gathered their things and set off once again. Lucas removed the ice cold water bottles from the bag and handed Alexander one. The cold water refreshed them and gave a small chill which they welcomed after a day of walking in the heat. Alexander led them to a bus terminal a few miles away, and when they arrived, they barely caught the last bus on their route. The driver, tired from a long day's work, paid no attention to Lucas and Alexander nor their lack of payment. They ate snack bars, kicked back, and relaxed, feeling the joy of another great day. The ride lasted quite a while, and once they disembarked, they still had a ways to walk.

By the time they reached the IHOP, both were exhausted, and they decided their efforts to create and write would be futile until they rested. So, they searched for a place to sleep nearby. They first tried a large patch of grass in a more inconspicuous area of a parking lot. Upon reaching it, however, they found the location unsatisfactory, so instead, they continued their search until Alexander spotted a parking garage off in the distance.

As they came closer, they could see the metal fence surrounding the parking garage and all the construction equipment aggregated in sporadic clusters. Alexander, shortly, found two fence sections chained together that he easily pulled apart at the bottom just wide enough for one person to squeeze through. They removed their backpacks and instruments, and Alexander wedged his way through first. Then, Lucas passed their things to him. Once all was through, Lucas shoved past the fence.

They took a gander at their surroundings. The parking garage was still under construction but appeared very close to finished.

Something about the rawness, the partial embodiment of this human construct appealed greatly to the both of them. On their way to the top level, the emptiness penetrated them deeply, precisely where unknown, but this could not prevent their marveling over an incomplete concept expected to provide so much. Before them, lives realized themselves, became, and in a token of gratitude, they held this concrete structure together.

At the top, the sky, no longer occluded, revealed its entirety. A great illuminated blackness rolled along its peaks and troughs above them, cloaking the world from any extraterrestrial observer. The city, like a child concealing herself beneath sheets, remained electric, alive, and determined. Lucas and Alexander could no longer give in to neither absolute nothingness nor ultimate brilliance. The only thing left for them this night were the majestic eclipses of dreams, so as soon as they prepped their pallet, they surrendered to sleep.

DAY TWO

A loud hissing, screeching sound rattled Lucas from his slumber. He strained against the adhesive holding his eye lids shut, but when he pried them open, he started at the sight of a man staring at him. Immediately, Lucas recognized the dress of a construction worker, and the timid expression on his face showed the uneasiness and confusion Lucas and Alexander's unexpected presence caused him. Lucas waved and greeted the man.

The man said quietly "Good morning. Do you mind if I work here?" He pointed to the concrete ledge nearby.

Lucas waved away the pleasantry and said "Of course, you need to work."

The man thanked Lucas and moved past him to the ledge he indicated and began working. Lucas laid back attempting to return to sleep, but the persistent noise made this impossible. He sat up, and again, he started at the sight of a man staring at him, but this time, the man approached from the other end and was still a distance away. He wore a dark blue uniform accented with a utility belt, and his hand rested on some large object protruding from his right hip. Lucas squinted to render the figure clearer, but was blinded by a bright glare from the man's left breast. Suddenly, Lucas realized the man approaching was a police officer.

Quickly, Lucas shook Alexander awake. "Dude! There's a cop coming!"

Alexander rolled over and threw his blanket over his head. Once more, Lucas shook him but more violently as his despair intensified. "Get up! There's a cop!"

Finally, Alexander rose to see what the fuss was all about. "A cop?" he asked as he rubbed his eyes.

"Yes!" Lucas exclaimed.

Alexander looked at the man with indifference. "So it is."

Fear and frustration washed over Lucas almost causing panic, but he managed to subdue the urge to run for his life. By the time he regained his composure, the police officer reached their pallet and stood at its edge towering over them.

"What are you two up to?" the officer asked.

Again, Lucas chose silent observation while Alexander replied "Just getting rest from our travels. I'm a traveler, and my friend here is on a mission to find truth. We just stopped here for the night, but we'll be on our way, soon."

"Interesting," the officer said, "where are you from?"

"A small country town here in Texas. Been all over Texas and some of Louisiana."

"Where are you headed?"

"Where ever the universe takes me, man. I'm following the vibes and the opportunities for growth."

The officer nodded, then shifted his attention to Lucas. "What are you searching for?"

Lucas inhaled deeply as he sorted his thoughts. "I'm trying to find out why we feel the need to create suffering on a mass scale, and I hope to discover a way to disprove this notion."

Silence enveloped them for a moment as the officer considered what Alexander and Lucas said. Lucas fidgeted his hands in the wrinkles of his blanket. Alexander studied the activity now permeating the environment, a stark contrast to the night before.

The officer cleared his throat. "Well, you guys are on the wrong part of town. Someone has been killing homeless people not far from here, and you two look like easy prey. Especially you." He pointed to Lucas. "I strongly suggest you find a better part of town."

"Wow, man!" Alexander remarked. "Good thing we stayed up here. We almost slept in a patch of grass near one of those parking lots."

"You need to be very careful around here," the officer said, "and you need to pack up. The men working aren't too comfortable with you up here."

Alexander and Lucas readily complied. As they collected their things, the officer stayed to insure they promptly left, and found himself chatting away with Alexander. Lucas kept quiet, focused solely on the task before him still wrestling a tempest within. Once they began their descent, the officer remained waiting to confirm their exit from the premise.

On the way down, Lucas and Alexander observed the men hard at work, and the endless glances cast their way. Sparks flew and a grinding sound screeched from a corner. The clash of metal on metal set the pace of their steps. At the bottom, the sun shone brightly through the opening of the exit like a great beacon beckoning them back to ultimate beauty.

The fence protecting the perimeter was now semipermeable thanks to a section pivoted on its hinges to allow for entry. Lucas and Alexander stepped out of the construction zone without further provocation save the unforeseen events of the day, and instantly, the garage, police officer, and construction crew passed into distant memory.

They headed for the IHOP eager to begin drafting their mission in poetry, lyric, or whatever other form it would take. Once it came into view, Lucas became apprehensive at the sight of a full parking lot and people waiting outside. They walked in to find a full waiting area and a concerned look from the hostess. It was hard to hear the hostess over the hubbub of the restaurant, but Lucas managed to ask for a table. Alexander asked if it would be possible for them to stay a while to write.

The manager, standing close by, inserted himself into the conversation inquiring exactly how long Alexander had in mind. When Alexander estimated a couple of hours, the manager frowned and shook his head, but Alexander persisted only causing the manager to forcefully deny their admission. After another failed attempt to persuade the manager, Alexander and Lucas left equally disappointed and frustrated.

"That's messed up!" Alexander exclaimed. "We had every right to be there. We have money."

"Perhaps, it is, but we would have also become a problem for them. They are packed, and we have all this stuff. We would get in the way of other customers" Lucas explained. "But, you shouldn't have told them we wanted to stay that long. Maybe, we could have gotten a table eventually."

"Yeah, they should've given us a table anyways!"

They decided to move on determined to find an alternative. At a traffic light about a quarter mile from the IHOP, a woman stood in a median holding up a sign broadcasting her need for change. Alexander suggested Lucas should ask her if there are any other diners in the area, so Lucas approached the woman trusting Alexander's sense of things. The woman, friendly enough, regretfully informed them no other diners were located anywhere near their current location. Furthermore, she warned gravely they were in "the wrong part of town". She listed off a few names of various drugs and noted several physical pleasures. "That's all that's here."

Lucas and Alexander thanked her for the information and took their leave. They walked along the frontage road of a major highway in a direction that felt fitting. In the distance, Alexander spotted a Walmart and suggested they try to acquire cigarettes from those around the entrance, and perhaps, they would receive more money as well.

They chose a spot roughly thirty feet from the entrance to lay down their equipment and for Lucas to rest while Alexander asked passersby for cigarettes. As Alexander importuned, Lucas entertained himself with playing his djembe. Ten minutes passed, and Alexander only managed to obtain one cigarette. Moved, however, by Lucas' drumming, he took a respite from his efforts to release the impulses coursing through his fingers.

The strings felt good beneath his fingertips as they danced across the frets from cord to cord, from major to minor. At least when he played, the reality Alexander envisioned manifested if only as the subtlest of visages and in that visage, ultimate bliss. Lucas, too, projected his reality but not as a competitor rather as a complement. Together, their realities harmonized to a greater whole.

A man, intrigued by the sounds emanating from an atypical source, approached to investigate. He stood close by leaning over to better hear. Soon, he began giving direction, telling Lucas to play quieter and Alexander to sing louder. Once adjustments were made, he gave encouraging remarks, then listened carefully bobbing his head to the beat. "Very nice," he commented.

At the conclusion of the song, Alexander asked the man for a cigarette, and the man responded by handing him a brand new pack. Alexander ecstatically thanked the man and accepted the generous gift. The man bade them goodbye and left encouraging words ringing in their ears.

All seemed well, so they decided to stick around a little longer. Suddenly, a woman emerged from the sea of cars and hastily strutted towards them. As she neared, Lucas and Alexander ceased playing. She looked at them with busy eyes and frequent rigid shifts in her posture.

"Hello, how are you guys?" She continued before they could answer. "Whatever Mary told you, forget about it. She doesn't know anything. This street is mine and my boyfriend's. We run this street."

Again, Alexander came to the rescue. "We just asked her if there were any diners around."

"Oh, okay. Well, Mary doesn't know anything. If you have questions, you ask me. This is my street."

"Yeah, no problem. We're just travelers passing through."

"Okay, good. Normally, I don't let anyone at this Walmart. This is where I work, but since you're just passing through, I'll allow it."

"Thanks. We're just about to move on anyways, so no worries."

"Well, you guys have a good day."

Alexander and Lucas repaid her salutation and watched as she slithered off back into the sea she emerged from. Slowly, the tension lessened, but the vibes the woman spewed disrupted all creative fluidity. To circumvent this obstruction, they decided to resume their journey.

As soon as they returned to the frontage road, their minds expanded, and the pain of constraining themselves dissolved into an encompassing feeling of healthiness. Their thoughts, now free, came bursting out.

"What was with that woman?" Lucas asked. "That was absurd. She runs this street? She's out of her mind."

"Yeah, that was pretty funny. No one can even own a street."

"She was completely territorial like an animal. She reminded me of a dog barking at me and following me as I walk about my neighborhood."

Alexander chuckled at the comparison. "Yeah man, that's a good analogy."

Lucas stopped in his tracks as a realization washed over him. "Wait." Lucas reached out his arm towards Alexander. "There's something more significant going on here."

"What do you mean?"

"She was more than a confused person. She is struggling with the most fundamental building blocks of life: love, acceptance, and community. That's why she claims that street as her own."

Alexander gave a look indicating he had no idea what Lucas was saying.

"You have to take into consideration the social hierarchy and how it affects us on those fundamental levels. Each level on the hierarchy comes with a social identity, and with that identity, roles and their rules." Lucas began walking again, and Alexander joined. "Even though each identity doesn't specify how much love, acceptance, and community you should receive, simply the division of people implies a significant disparity exists or should exist, and then, we begin to allocate to ourselves the love, acceptance, and community in only the proportions we believe fit our status. We only receive the love, acceptance, and community we think we deserve, and our position on the social hierarchy influences how much we think we deserve.

"So, I think she has become fed up with her status because she feels it doesn't allow her to fulfill those fundamental needs adequately enough, and furthermore, something prevents her from conforming to the current paradigm in her pursuit to elevate her status to justify her receiving more love, acceptance, and community. Perhaps, she has lost faith in the current paradigm. Anyhow, she decides to abandon the general paradigm to create her own; she disregards any previous claims of possession of that street and claims it for herself. Possession over the street, in her paradigm, elevates her status enabling her to allow herself to receive greater portions of love, acceptance, and community.

"Maybe, she does receive more from her boyfriend, but beyond him and perhaps a small few of others, however, no one adhering to the general paradigm will give her anything at all. Instead, she will be bombarded with hate, disapproval, and ostracism for defying the paradigm, especially since she defied it through means abhorred by society. Therefore, her apparent success with those few will merely act as an illusion. When the people of the general paradigm move into re-assimilate her, she will lose everything and be worse off than before because she will be given an even lower status."

Alexander looked less confused, but his eyes betrayed a struggle yet resolved. "I see what you're saying now, but I don't see why people would act that way. If what you say is true, then why wouldn't people abandon the social hierarchy and just allow themselves to receive more love, acceptance, and community?"

"Because their conditioning of how the social world is has too great a hold on their imaginations and thus their autonomy of their perception of reality. They cannot fathom a different way, a different system. They don't see that love, acceptance, and community are completely separate from the social hierarchy. They don't see that there is no need to fabricate a higher status like this woman did to get their needs met. They don't understand that it is the current paradigm itself that prevents their needs from being met. They fail, as this woman surely will, because they merely recreate another manifestation of the same inadequate paradigm on too smaller a scale to resist re-assimilation into the broader system.

"If they want to truly overcome the limitations the social hierarchy places on their reception of love, acceptance, and community, they must abandon the current paradigm entirely and dream up a new, transcendent one. This new paradigm would assimilate the old to it, not it to the old. Until they do that, they will just remain criminals like this woman, but what's worse, the current paradigm creates this criminality"

"I wonder what kind of world that will be."

"A much more beautiful world."

Alexander nodded vehemently. "Definitely."

"But, I guess the only entity that has the power to claim a street is the government."

"They can think they own a street," Alexander clarified "but humanity can't own the earth. Nature is for everyone and everything."

"Hey, if we can't own the earth, can we own anything? I mean that must be where the concept of possession originated. Before we could own what we created, we must have 'owned' nature, first nature that is."

"That's a good question, but I think the answer is simple. No, we can't own anything. This false notion that we can possess anything causes so much suffering and chaos. Wars are fought over possessions, even religious wars or wars over ideas. It all comes back to possession, man."

"How do religious and ideological wars originate from possession?"

"Oh, man, that's simple too. Wars over ideas start when people try to possess truth and thought. They are trying to claim the mental world as theirs, but the mental world is just like nature. Well, it is a part of nature. You can't own it."

"Now, I've never thought of that! That's an excellent point. So if possession causes suffering like wars, starvation, poverty, poor health, and degradation of individual worth, then why do we maintain such a damaging concept? That's the real conundrum here. Why are we hurting ourselves?"

"Okay, so that's not so simple. I guess most still think it's a good thing. Maybe, they don't see the suffering it creates or they just don't care or maybe, it's the best they have to work with. That's all I can think of."

"Can you hand me a snack bar, please?" Lucas asked as he stopped and turned his back to Alexander.

Alexander untied the plastic bag and fished out a chocolate chip Cliff Bar. He retied the bag and handed the bar to Lucas.

"Thanks." As he tore open the wrapper, Lucas commented "Because people think they can own the means to produce food like this and require payment for it, slavery still exists. If you really think about it, the chains that fetter us to someone or something or some idea are built from possession." Lucas bit a chunk out of the snack bar.

"What do you mean by that?"

"Well, besides the fact that slavery itself is an act of possession, the only way it can exist is if someone has the power to create it, which only comes from one's possession of the means to life and happiness. Because possession exists and only a select few hold possession over the means to life and happiness, those who don't, have no choice but to submit to those who do. It's quite an enigma."

"Yeah man, how do you escape possession? It's rooted deeply in everything."

"I'm not sure. Again, you would have to create a whole new paradigm that's actually feasible and minimally discomforting to transition to. You have to fathom the unfathomable. Developing the capacity to do *that* is the evolutionary direction we need to take if we want to create such a world, but does humanity really want to?"

"Looks like most don't. That's really sad, man."

They trekked on in the heat of the afternoon sun which shone brightly overhead. Every couple of minutes, Lucas wiped the sweat from his eyes already numb to the salty sting. He noticed this nuisance never seemed to bother Alexander and realized Alexander's bandana served a purpose beyond mere aesthetic appeal. Lucas felt his clothes growing heavy and their grasp tightening obstructing the fluidity of his limbs, however, he did not feel constrained nor restrained. His body and its movements had simply become different, and he pushed on without concern. Both drank large quantities of water, and eventually, depleted their supply.

A Fiesta store came into view, and Lucas suggested they buy a gallon jug of water like the one Alexander had the first time they met. Alexander expressed uneasiness at the prospect of adding so much weight and bulk but surrendered to its great logical appeal.

Outside the entrance, picnic tables were placed near a small concession stand. They picked a free table and set their things down. Alexander chose to watch their equipment and attempt to obtain more money while Lucas went inside to purchase water. As Lucas made his way to the entrance, he threw away the empty water bottles the man gave them and the snack bar wrapper into a trashcan.

Once inside, Lucas navigated the vast aisles stocked with superfluous amounts of food, drinks, and various other merchandises with familiarity and blasé, but something within stirred uncomfortably. Eventually, he found the water aisle and meandered between his options. Lucas focused on the shape and stability of the plastic jug searching for something easily attached to their packs while being able to withstand the hardships of travel. After great care and testing, he selected one and proceeded to the checkout.

The lines were long, so Lucas had to wait as the customers before him piled their groceries on the conveyor belt and the cashier scanned each item one by one. The methodical movement of the cashier's hands seemed to hypnotize Lucas; his gaze never strayed from the repetitious process. A bag of frozen vegetables, a pair of luscious pork chops, a gallon of milk, a bag of chips, a loaf of bread, a two liter bottle of soda, fresh apples and bananas all passed in a steady stream past his eyes until he could bear it no longer.

He closed his eyes and thought coaxingly to himself: *It's only temporary.* When his turn arrived, he hurriedly slammed down the jug and handed over the payment. Quickly, he took his receipt and rushed out the door.

Alexander sat at their table smoking and enjoying an orange. Nothing appeared to trouble him as though he were oblivious to any and every adversity. Lucas in his turmoil found himself loathing yet enjoying this coolness, this calmness. A fire had sparked in him.

"Let's get out of here. I can't stand it."

Alexander, realizing the shift in Lucas' mood, treaded carefully. "Sure, man. No problem."

Before they left, Alexander tied the water jug to Lucas' pack after he insisted he take on the extra weight for the moment at least, and as soon as he could, Lucas started walking. They crossed through a parking lot on the side of the Fiesta heading back to the edge of the frontage road. Halfway across, the water jug slid down hitting Lucas in the thigh. They stopped to make adjustments, but it proved a more difficult task than anticipated.

While they struggled to perfect attaching the water jug, a Chinese man in the distance called out to them. They looked around until they found him a little further down their heading. The man held up a black nylon laptop bag and gestured his inquiry if they would like to reappropriate it for their water jug. Eager for anything that might help, Alexander and Lucas ceased their struggle to give the man's solution a try.

When they came near, the man explained how he found the bag and had no use for it himself. He would rather see it put to some good use than be thrown away, and any use he might give it could not possibly stand up to that of Alexander and Lucas. They gratefully accepted the gift and promised to use it well.

As the man made to leave, Alexander asked if he could give them a ride just a little way down the road. Unfortunately, the man's vehicle belonged to the city, and thus he did not have the authority to use it in such a way. Alexander smiled and thanked the man and told him not to worry; he has already done so much. They waved as the man drove off in the direction they traveled.

The water jug fit awkwardly in the bag due to its bulk, but they decided to allow it a chance to serve the purpose for which it was given. Once Lucas acclimated to the shift in weight distribution, they continued walking.

They walked for another mile when Lucas caught sight of a Chinese buffet. The hunger had set in a while ago with all its discomforts, and the trip to Fiesta only exacerbated the sensation. Now, food, substantial food commanded his focus and desires. He pleaded they go and stuff their stomachs to kill the hunger for good. Alexander, hungry himself, gave no resistance, and they redirected their heading straight for the restaurant. Images and smells and tastes of past indulgences flooded Lucas' mind. His mouth filled with saliva, and his entire being urged itself towards the entrance at a quickened pace.

The Chinese restaurant was located in a plain shopping center built of squares and rectangles with flat faces. The parking lot had very few cars, and signs of life were limited. The big wooden double doors leading to the great buffet of all you can eat delicacies imprinted themselves on the retinas of Lucas' eyes like a great monument or a majestic scenery. To Lucas, heaven was just beyond those doors.

Right as they entered, an onslaught of scents titillated their olfactory bulbs exponentially greater than predicted. The old man behind the checkout counter greeted them warmly showing no concern for their equipment and instruments. Then, a waitress directed them to a table adjacent to a long booth on one side and chairs on the other. The tables on either side were unoccupied, so they had plenty of room for their things. The waitress brought water, and they raced to the food.

Lucas stacked food as tall as the plate could hold, peppered steak, green beans, and broccoli, all combined in quite a colorful display. Alexander's plate, too, was piled high. They sat down and began stuffing their faces with the most superb mixtures of flavors. Both underestimated the magnitude of their hunger. Once adequately satiated to allow for conversation, they sat back and washed down the remnants of masticated heaven with water.

"Dude," Lucas started, "this is delicious! Totally worth it."

"Yeah man, I'm glad you had this idea." Alexander rubbed his belly happily.

"Being so hungry makes this all the better. This has to be the best Chinese food I've ever had, and there's so much of it!"

"And, they have some pretty awesome looking desserts."

"I know!" Lucas exclaimed his agreement. "I have to give that cake a try, and that fruit would be so good right now."

They stood up together and headed to the desserts and fruit despite their unfinished plates, though they intended to finish those as well. Lucas began picking the pieces he favored most of the honeydew, cantaloupe, watermelon, and red grapes. Alexander honed in first on the almost perfectly sliced squares of layered chocolate mousse on chocolate cake on chocolate mousse on chocolate cake topped with a gelatinous sugar coating. Then, Alexander moved toward the cream puffs and the other pastries that caught his eyes.

He stacked his dessert plate. Lucas took a slice of the square mousse cake and a cream puff, but he didn't want to over indulge.

They walked back to their table.

Alexander pick up a cream puff with his fingers, and as he bit into it, he let out a hum of satisfaction. "So good."

Lucas tried the square cake and found himself humming in kind. "Oh, yeah. *This* is great." He took another bite and smiled with pleasure. "Thanks for being her with me and taking me on this journey."

"No problem, man. I'm glad we're doing this."

"Me, too. I can't think of a better companion." Lucas smiled at Alexander then returned to his cake.

"Thanks, man." Alexander smiled back.

"You know, this place doesn't look busy, and they have all that food. I really hope they don't just throw it away."

"They probably will. That's what restaurants do."

"That's a shame! You could feed so many people with all this food. I don't know how they could just throw it away. If I owned a restaurant, I would give out food at the end of the day. There's no way I could live with myself if I just tossed it all, especially after being out here. I mean there's so much opportunity to do good here. We could set up some sort of food dispensary. We could take a step towards making the civilization we've been envisioning. We could help facilitate the realizations of so many potentialities. We could help people be the best they can be!"

"Yeah man, I completely agree. If we owned this joint, we could change so many lives, and if every restaurant joined us, no one would ever go hungry again. We could start a revolution to feed. It's a beautiful thought, man. People need to wake up and see what's important."

"I think it could be done easily enough. It would take a bit more effort and time, maybe some money. Heck! We could even have the government or some charity subsidize the operation. That way we ensure it doesn't harm the restaurant owners to take care of their fellow humans. Dude! Why hasn't anyone done this already?"

"I don't know, man. Money is usually the problem, and legal issues."

"If those are the only thing stopping us from taking care of our people, we should feel ashamed of ourselves. We are letting a system we created and completely control stop us from doing what we need to do. That's like letting a hammer stop us from driving a nail!"

Alexander burst out laughing not sure which was funnier Lucas' analogy or how seriously he said it. He settled down and said "When you put it like that, it seems pretty absurd."

"It is absurd! It's completely asinine to hinder such necessary acts. Acts like these are what really hold civilization together. Hinder these, and you destroy civilization."

"Yeah man, you have a good point, but let's think about us for a moment. I'd really like to take some of this food with us. Do you think we could get a to-go box?"

"I doubt it. Buffets don't usually allow it, but I'll go ask."

Lucas rose from the table and approached a waitress. His question was immediately met with a stern but apologetic no. Lucas decided not to push the matter and returned to the table.

"Well, she said no. We better eat as much as we can."

They went back to gulping down the remaining food on their dinner plates, setting their desserts aside and once finished, served themselves seconds. They ate until they felt they would burst. Then, they tested the veracity of this sensation with more sweet treats and fresh fruits. Both were quite stuffed and grateful for a different kind of stomach pain.

"I'm serious about taking food with us." Alexander continued.

"But, we have no place to put the food."

"We can wrap it up in napkins and put it in our pockets or one of our bags."

"No! That's too messy." Lucas retorted not yet ready to allow himself to behave to such an extreme.

"It'd be fine, man. I'll wrap it up really well."

"Look, you can if you want to, but I don't want to be a part of it. It doesn't feel right to me."

"Alright, man. Don't worry about it."

Lucas poked at the pieces of fruit left on his plate taking a bite everyone once in a while. Alexander finished eating the pastries on his plate. Suddenly, an idea occurred to Alexander.

"Hey, take a look at all the people around us right now. All their minds are closed in one way or another. Our minds, too. I have an idea to open up all our minds."

Alexander captured Lucas' curiosity, evident in his eager "What?"

"You see those two tables?" Alexander pointed to the two tables to their right currently unoccupied. "We should clear them off and meditate on them."

Lucas looked aghast and remained silent. As he imagined himself performing this act, it seemed as though two realities collided before his eyes, and he was still trying to make sense of the vibrant display. Finally, he managed to utter a silent, shaky "What?"

"Yeah, man. We should meditate on those tables. It will open our minds and everyone else's."

For twenty minutes, Lucas wrestled with the idea. He found fear to be the foundation to his refusal, and though the act appeared ridiculous, he wanted to overcome this strong fear building in him. Alexander continued to coax and persuade Lucas seeing the internal struggle play out before him. Eventually, Lucas gathered the strength to accept the challenge.

"Great!" Alexander's excitement rose. "Alright, we will get up, move everything on our table to the same side, and move the chairs to the same sides also. All at exactly the same time. When we meditate, we have to keep our eyes closed, no matter what, until someone touches us. Also, the goal is to remain completely humble, so we can't laugh. We have to remain serious."

"Got it. When do we start?"

"Now."

Alexander stood, and Lucas inhaled deeply as he rose. They walked to their respective tables not more than five feet away. Lucas watched Alexander closely ensuring he did exactly as he did when he did it. First, they moved the two chairs out from the side facing the rest of the restaurant. One went to the right; the other to the left. Their movements so far were in perfect synchrony, and they began to attract the attention of the other diners nearby. Next, they pushed the utensil and condiment holders to the right hand corner. Lucas locked eyes with Alexander for a moment. Then, each turned around facing the inner restaurant, and slid back onto the tables. They crossed their legs, positioned their hands, and closed their eyes.

To Lucas, all appeared surreal. With his eyes closed he could almost believe it was all just a crazy dream, but after only a minute, the old man's voice came boring into his ears. Fear had already excreted its caustic fluids from the start, but somehow, it commanded a whole new intensity unlike anything Lucas had ever felt before. His heart raced as though *it* had enough of this charade and would not stick around for the aftermath. Urged to run away, his body seemed to abandon him as if the dissonance of wills between body and mind became too great for the body, but he pleaded and implored for his body to trust him. Finally, his body acquiesced.

The old man continued to yell, "You can't do that here! This is not your house. You can't do that!" as he slammed his hand on the tables they sat on. Customers looked on appalled. Some video recorded them on their phones.

Alexander opened his eyes, though he was not touched. He felt deep respect for the old man and could not bear to distress him any longer. When he looked to Lucas, he saw his eyes were still closed. A smile spread midway up his cheeks, but vanished almost as quickly as it appeared. Lucas was doing well, and he was proud of him.

Finally, the old man, still yelling, lightly poked Lucas on his right shouldered, and immediately, Lucas lifted his heavy lids revealing a serenity in his eyes. They slid off the tables, and the old man ceased his roaring. As they moved slowly and calmly to gather their things, the old man stood close by ushering them along. The old man led them to the cash register, and they paid the bill leaving a nice tip. Lucas hurriedly pocketed the remaining change, and then, they pushed through the large, wooden double doors to embrace the piercing rays of a setting sun.

Neither spoke until they returned to the frontage road. The silent walk allowed each to savor the experiences just had and the energies it created within and without. Lucas broke the silence with a mighty, joyful howl.

"I'm alive!" Lucas shouted. "I did that and didn't die!"

"Of course, you're alive. Why wouldn't you be?"

"Think about it, man. I was terrified, but why; what was there to be terrified of? All we did was break a social norm. Nothing physically dangerous occurred. And, that's exactly the point! The fear came from the deep-seated conditioning that if I act different to an extreme, I will be ostracized from society, lose all my social ties, and ultimately, lose everything because I receive everything from this social web. At least, that's how the conditioning goes. But, Look! I'm alive and nothing has changed. This means I can be who I truly am and not die! Maybe even thrive!"

"Yeah, man! You have to break free of that conditioning. You have to be you, man."

Suddenly, the profundity of Lucas' experience penetrated beneath his intellect to his emotions and the adrenaline still coursing through him compounded the impact. He burst out laughing and could not stop, though the ecstasy felt too fantastic for him to truly try. Alexander had no defenses capable of preventing such a contagious laugh from flowing through him as well, and he, too, began laughing uncontrollably. They stumbled and swayed from side to side clenching their abdomens and gasping for air.

Eventually, they settled down, and Alexander continued. "That conditioning was created to domesticate us and keep us in line. It's just another way to keep us in slavery. Like you said before, it's one of the ways people lose their autonomy."

"Of course! I didn't realize it before because I was still trapped. Even I don't completely have my autonomy. I'm still chained, man! I need to break free from the remaining bonds, and this is one of them. I'm still afraid to be me!"

Alexander looked over Lucas from head to toe and nodded. "Alright. I have a plan, but you have to do whatever I tell you to do."

The hairs on the back of Lucas' neck stood up as the prospect of facing himself further gave rise to the fear again. "What are you going to tell me to do?"

"I don't know yet, but when the time comes, I'll tell you to do something that I know will help you break out of your conditioning. You have to trust me."

"Okay, however, if I feel it has bad vibes, I don't have to do it. That's my only condition. I want to face this fear, so you have to trust that I won't try to run from whatever it is you tell me to do."

Alexander smiled and reached out a hand. "You got yourself a deal."

They shook hands to finalize the agreement, and both felt a new surge of purpose. Finally, Alexander had a method to help Lucas find his way back to himself. He knew the opportunity would present itself when they both were ready.

Lucas felt that this agreement embodied everything he sought on his journey; that everything led to this seemingly by design. He felt that, soon, he would become what he needed despite the fear projecting differently.

Alexander suddenly exclaimed "I know of the perfect place for us right now on the other side of town. Let's catch a bus and head over there."

They only needed to walk another block to reach an empty bus stop, and they sat down to wait for the next bus. Lucas knew nothing of bus routes nor how they would arrive at the destination Alexander had in mind, but he trusted Alexander implicitly to get them there. In his comfort, he allowed his mind to wander to more pertinent matters.

Lucas leaned back on the bench and stretched out his legs. As he stared at his shoes, he said "All this thinking and talking, man, about such radically different perceptions of reality and ways of life, what does it amount to if I'm still scared of myself? How can I speak these things or act on them if I still can't face myself?"

Alexander, watching a dark cloud slowly engulf Lucas, attempted to reach through to him. "Hey man, it's one thing to think and another to do, but you have to think before you act. That's what you're doing right now. You're becoming aware of your fear, and then, you will face it and overcome it. I know you will, and when you do that, man, nothing will stop you. We are all scared of ourselves. It's a part of the conditioning."

"But, what am I really afraid of? I'm not afraid of being different or being made an outcast because I'm different."

Alexander lit himself a cigarette. To his surprise, Lucas asked for one. He handed him one and the lighter. Lucas lit it and inhaled deeply.

"Yeah, I know." Lucas said noticing Alexander's surprise. "I don't believe in this, but in moderation and how rarely I smoke, cigarettes are harmless enough." He handed the lighter back to Alexander. "Besides, I trust myself not to get caught up in smoking."

"There you go, man. That's the kind of trust you need in yourself for everything."

"But it's not that I don't trust myself. Sure, I still don't completely, but that's not the heart of it. I'm scared that underneath all we've been talking about and what I plan to do about it, at my core, there's really nothing. I'm scared this is all meaningless because in the end, I can't do anything because there's no substance inside me to back it all up. I feel like I'm falling in an abyss of nothingness."

Alexander looked down at his hands and then at his guitar. "Yeah. I know what you mean, but hey, you only feel that way because you are judging yourself on a value system that's not yours. It doesn't even apply to you."

"What do you mean?"

"It all goes back to our conditioning. We're taught what is supposed to be valuable and anything that doesn't resemble this is considered unvaluable or less valuable. That nothingness inside you is really something, but it just doesn't match your conditioned understanding of value. You can't see it as a substance because you are blinded by a value system imposed on you that doesn't even include your essence. You have to forget that value system if you are to see yourself."

Seemingly out of nowhere, a bus pulled up to the stop. Lucas had been so engrossed in thought he hardly paid any attention to his surroundings. They quickly gathered their belongings and boarded the bus. Once they found seats and set down their things, Lucas inserted the fare in the collection apparatus near the driver. He was grateful to have received change at the Chinese restaurant.

When Lucas sat down, Alexander continued "You have to create your own value system and explore what *something* that nothingness really is."

"I know, but in order to do that I have to risk throwing everything valuable away. I have to pass through the floor of the existent value system, but I'm afraid that only an abyss lies beneath and it will only consume me and I'll disappear forever. I want to face this. I want to dive head first, but I'm trembling on the diving board and am about to turn back.

"It's as though I am asking if I truly have a soul or really do exist and I'm terrified I'll find that I, in fact, don't have one and don't exist. I'm not sure I could handle finding that out."

Alexander closed his eyes, then slowly opened them. "Bro, these are some scary thoughts, but how do you know you're throwing anything away? How do you know you're not really falling but flying?"

"I don't know. Everything is ambiguous and uncertain. For all I know, I could be walking into an Eden of being, but I don't know. I'm just afraid I'll destroy myself simply by being me."

"But if you're not yourself, you will destroy yourself. You may feel safe and have things and be a part of a community that loves and accepts you, but if you're not truly you, it will all be a lie and a betrayal of self. I know you could never be happy that way."

"And I'm not happy with how things are now. If I continue to live life this way, I'll condemn myself to misery, but if I give being myself a try, I could become happy or be thrown further into misery. I couldn't handle any deeper misery."

"You have nothing to lose by being yourself, man. You said it yourself. You only have happiness to gain. This being thrown into a deeper misery is nonsense! It's the conditioning talking. Remember talking about how people think their salvation is their destruction. That's what you are doing right now. You have to fight the conditioning. You have to love yourself."

Lucas turned to look out the window. He enjoyed watching the buildings, trees, and pedestrians pass by at their different rates. How things small and close passed quickly and things large and distant passed slower. Everything appeared to flow past as though a great current swept them all away. He turned back to Alexander.

"You're right. I have nothing to lose except fear itself. For so long, I have lived in fear without realizing it, and now, I must have the final battle. The last hook fear has in me is the fear of living without fear. If I face this and live as I truly am, loving myself all the while, fear will no longer stop me, but transform into a force that propels me further. When this happens, the conditioning will no longer have any control over me. Fear is nothing more than the conditioning fighting back against my fighting it."

"Exactly, man! You got it!"

"But, if only knowing that made it easier…"

"Nah, man. There's no way to make it easier. There's only knowing what the struggle is for. All you can do is figure out why, then you become strong enough to endure anything."

Alexander went to ask the bus driver what route would most efficiently deliver them to the place he had in mind. The bus driver informed him of the stop he should disembark at and the next bus to board. Only one transfer would be required. He thanked the driver and sat back down.

Lucas remained silently deep in thought for the rest of the ride, and when they reached their stop, he allotted the least amount of focus to getting off the bus. They had made their way to a buffer between the urban downtown and the suburbs. The next bus stop was surrounded by shopping centers that overflowed into the surrounding area, and houses lay just beyond. They decided to sit on their bags in a patch of grass.

A shirtless man with red leather pants shouted from the bus stop bench. His wife, dressed in a superhero costume, laughed hysterically. The man, jumped up and continued shouting unintelligibly in a thick Irish accent. When he noticed Lucas and Alexander, he strode over to them to investigate.

"Hey, do you know how to play those things, lads, or do you carry them to look cool?"

Alexander responded coolly, "Yeah, man. We know how to play them."

"Well then, play us something! Let's hear it."

Alexander and Lucas found no reason to refuse, so they prepared to play. Lucas felt uncomfortable with the man so close to them, and alcohol vapor stung his nose. Alexander, however, appeared to like the man. Once they began playing, the man jumped up and shouted in delight, startling Lucas but not interfering with his drumming. After they completed a song, the man announced loudly "These boys deserve a beer," and he stumbled back to where he came from. When he returned, he held a can of beer and vehemently offered it with a proud countenance.

Alexander gladly accepted the beer and thanked the man. Then, the man returned to his wife, and together, they walked away, leaving all in their wake. Alexander opened the beer and drank as he watched the couple disappear into the night. He handed the beer to Lucas, and they shared the beer savoring the moment together. A while later, the bus arrived.

Lucas switched his attention from the moving scenery to Alexander. "You know, I'm not just afraid that there is no substance in me. I'm also afraid of what is there. I'm scared of my flaws, my bad characteristics. They hang over my head like nuclear bombs that could be dropped at any time destroying everything without warning. It's petrifying."

"Hey man, that's just the developing you. I don't think it's as bad as you fear."

Lucas interrupted. "Yes it is! Look at my family. All of their pain and mishaps and wrong turns was ultimately caused by themselves. Look at literature. There are tons of tragedies about people's flaws leading them to self-destruction. It's as though humans are destined to destroy themselves if they don't constantly check themselves out of fear. This is a common theme in religions as well. It's like the great human fallibility!"

"Yeah, but it's still not as bad as all of that makes it out to be. You're looking at all those as loses and destructions, but they aren't. Those 'tragedies' don't take away from you but give you so much. They teach you something. Each and every one of those 'tragedies' offers a lesson if you are willing to accept it, and these lessons are vital to your growth. Without them, you become stagnant. They give you the pieces of yourself you've been longing for all along.

"They only become destructive when you choose not to learn from them. Then, they become cycles that begin to shape your life. Your family still feels the same pain and still makes the same mistakes because they haven't accepted the lessons from one or more tribulations. It's the same with all humans. We shouldn't fear making mistakes. We should strive to learn from them and to never become unwilling to learn."

"But, there is a price for each lesson. You do lose something. In relationships it's a person. In finance, money. In injury, health. I don't want to lose anything. I'd rather I learn without having to pay a price."

"And you can until you reach the limit of human experience. If you want to go beyond and explore the frontier, though, you must be willing to trade yourself for the unknown, or you never will learn anything. I don't like the word price. I prefer to look at it not as paying, giving up piece of yourself for something outside of yourself, but an exchange, trading one piece of yourself for a different piece of yourself. It's like we have a finite existence, and if we want to expand in one direction we must take from another. Like a moving island.

"What we lose in the exchange, only we lose. What we gain spreads to the human collective, so others can learn without having to exchange anything because we already have. I say try your best to learn from the exchanges already made, but don't run away from exchange itself. One day, you could make an exchange that can help us all, and that will only happen if you chose to face it and accept the privilege to add to humanity's experience."

"I just wish it wasn't so scary. When you're making the exchange, you never know what you are going to receive. That uncertainty drives me crazy!"

"It's that uncertainty that gives life its thrill. Things wouldn't be, well, the way they are without it. It's the way of existence, and it doesn't have to be seen as scary. You can choose to look at it as a challenge or an adventure. You just have to trust you are a part of the universe with a distinct role to play and that the universe will take care of itself."

The bus came to a halt, and Alexander rose. "This is our stop." They gathered their things and stepped off the bus.

Silence and the cool touch of night greeted them. Across the street, a six story building stood by a large field of tall grass scarcely ornamented with trees. To their left about a block away, a strip center illuminated an empty parking lot save one cluster of cars out front a small bar. Their right revealed a path to somnambulant planned communities. Behind them, the whisper of moving cars from the distant highway floated on the breeze.

Lucas insisted they find a place to sleep before he passed out, so they headed to the field. Three trees grew in a triangular pattern with the hypotenuse being no more than forty feet. This spot appealed most to Alexander, and he led them to its center. They unraveled their bedding and made their pallet, hidden by the tall grass.

As soon as Lucas laid down his head, he drifted off to sleep. Alexander, however, stared at the stars, unusually bright, piercing through the smog, and pondered how a star might make itself shine brighter. Eventually, he, too, succumbed to the great cosmic will.

DAY THREE

Something was amiss. He flew over the Pacific Ocean with mechanical wings strapped to his back. The sun's blinding rays showered him and the clouds beneath. The ocean a distant plane. The blue sky seemed limitless. But there it was, this sharp stinging on his chest. Suddenly, his wings snapped off, and he started to free fall. He floundered in a panic, but soon realized there was nothing he could do. He settled himself, so he faced the ocean shooting up at him. Then, he rolled over to watch the sky float away. In the final half of his fall, he turned on his side to admire the horizon which remained the same. He hit the water. Above him, giant ripples rushed outward from his point of impact. The rear chased the foremost but never met despite its eternal pursuit.

Lucas sat straight up and a sharp sting pulsed through his scalp. Around him, acorns speckled the pallet. Where Alexander slept, only ruffled blankets and acorns presented themselves. He scanned his surroundings but found no trace of Alexander.

"Good morning!" Alexander called from a nearby tree.

Lucas found Alexander and replied, "What's with all these acorns?"

"Gravity, man." Alexander said with a smile on his face. "Glad you finally woke up."

"Yeah, me too. I was having the strangest dream."

Alexander climbed down from his perch and jumped to the ground. He walked to the pallet where Lucas sat. "We have a lot to do today."

Lucas rubbed his scalp then emerged from the comfort of his blanket. "Well, I have to pee, first."

"Perfect! What a great way to start the day. I want you to climb that tree," Alexander pointed to the tree growing furthest away of the three, "and pee off the top of it."

Taken aback but remembering the agreement he made, Lucas decided to do as Alexander suggested. When he approached the tree, he found the branches too high to reach, so he went back to their pallet to retrieve one of the thicker ropes. He threw the rope up intending for the rope to wrap around the branch of his choosing, but it failed to make contact. He tried again, but this time, not enough of the rope extended over the branch for him to grab. Again, he tried, and again, he failed.

"You're doubting yourself. Look how rigid you are. That's taking away from the force of your throw. Trust in your body's ability and let go of it. Release the tension and let it flow."

Lucas tried once more and almost managed to send enough rope over the branch. He took a deep breath and relaxed his muscles. He cocked his arm then shot it forward releasing the bundle of rope at the calculated angle. The rope soared up and over the branch landing on its midpoint. Finally, Lucas did it. He grabbed the other end and tied the two parts together. Once the knot tightened properly, Lucas grabbed both strands of rope, climbed, and pulled himself up onto the branch.

At the top, he could see the empty field, the passing cars, the strip center, now more densely populated, the highway, the neighborhoods, and an IHOP in the distance he did not see the night before. After careful consideration, Lucas picked the side facing the center of the field. A nervousness set in. He was not sure if he could be seen, though he thought the canopy provided enough cover. Deciding this fear must be overcome, Lucas began to urinate.

A breeze swayed the tree and had a refreshing appeal. He felt good, free in the exaltation of this humanly act. In this moment, the shame of such bestiality transformed into a prideful celebration of existence. He could imagine no better way to meet the body's needs. When he finished, he let out a rapturous howl then climbed back down.

"That felt great!" Lucas exclaimed as he walked back to the pallet.

"I knew it would. Isn't it great to be a living creature with all of its biological processes and to be a part of a whole ecosystem of other creatures and the elements?"

"What felt best was that I was embracing my being with pride instead of hiding it. I declared that it's okay to be a biological organism."

"Exactly, man. Humanity has tried to run from the very nature of themselves. It's unhealthy to be ashamed of our nature. Now, we must fight."

Lucas' excitement turned to anxiety, "What? Why?"

"Don't worry, man. It's just some friendly sparing."

They moved from the pallet until only grass surrounded them. Then, it started. They circled each other keeping their distance, arms waving, feet sliding. Lucas stepped forward and issued a light jab. Missing he stepped back. Alexander kicked to the left of Lucas. Lucas moved back in to land a punch on Alexander's left shoulder, as Alexander countered with a kick to Lucas' right leg. They returned to circling each other.

Lucas' breathing became heavy with the exertion and the lack of caloric intake for the day. He decided to stop the dancing which required so much of his body and focus his energy, instead, on a close-quarter's entanglement. He charged colliding his shoulder into Alexander's hip. Alexander resisted the tackle, but eventually, they both fell to the ground. Each tried to pin the other, however, their mutual efforts forced them to roll around with neither gaining the advantage. Finally, Lucas retreated after breaking free.

"Good," Alexander said between gasps of air. "Now, let's fight with our eyes closed."

Lucas laughed but closed his eyes nonetheless. Listening to each other's footsteps, they located one another and kicked and punched the air. Alexander managed to hit Lucas' arm. Lucas responded by throwing himself at Alexander, and again, they rolled about the ground. They fought to overpower the other, but still, neither succeeded. Lucas broke free once more and retreated. Circling again with their eyes open, they stared into each other's souls watching the fire burn in both. Alexander smiled and stood up straight.

"We've done enough. Now, follow me."

Alexander sprinted off to the tree he climbed earlier and grabbed hold of the lowest branch to pull himself onto it. After a second's hesitation, Lucas pursued at top speed and climbed onto the same branch, following Alexander to the top of the tree. Once they reached the top, they sat on their respective branches.

"I want you to embrace the trunk of the tree until you have become one with the tree. Don't let go until then."

The bark felt rough against his cheek and fingers, sharp edges stinging, but Lucas pressed his body as hard as he could against the tree trunk and closed his eyes. As he sat there with deep, heavy breaths, he tried to extend his consciousness into the tree. Letting go of all his thoughts and emotions, he welcomed in the essence of the tree.

After ten minutes, Alexander asked "Are you one?"

Another five minutes of silence passed before Lucas responded. "I don't know. I'm trying, but I only feel myself."

"Exactly. You are the tree; well, in a way. You and the tree are both expressions of the universe. You are connected because you are the universe. The same goes for everyone and everything. We are all connected, and to understand the existence of people and things, we only need to look within."

Lucas remained hugging the tree while he digested Alexander's words. "We are all pieces of infinity infinitely connected through our essence, the essence of the universe."

Alexander returned to the pallet leaving Lucas to his thoughts and started cleaning off the acorns. A moment later, Lucas climbed down to join him. After cleaning the pallet of acorns, they sat and ate the rest of the oranges.

Once they finished eating, Lucas decided to change clothes and asked Alexander where he should change. When Alexander told him to change where he was, his insecurities made him anxious, and the idea of undressing in public embarrassed him. Nonetheless, Lucas realized this, too, was a fear he needed to face, so he picked out clean clothes and changed.

Lucas was only naked for a second, but to him, it felt as if he had defied an entire society's supreme law. He felt criminal and terrified of the punishment to come. After he put on his underwear, he shoved his body into the other articles, and then sat down and scanned the area for trouble. No danger could be detected.

Eventually, they decided to pack up and attempt to gain entry into the new IHOP. Both still hungered for greater sustenance than the oranges provided, but Lucas particularly craved coffee and the opportunity to finally gather all he learned into an ultimate medium.

The walk covered a minimal distance, and when the IHOP came clearly into view, they were delighted to see a sparse parking lot. At the hostess' stand, a young woman greeted them and directed them to a table in an area that could accommodate their belongings. She handed them menus and pleasantly informed them a waiter would be right with them. This was an encouraging beginning.

When their waiter came, they ordered coffee and asked for more time to look at the menu. Lucas counted their money and confirmed they had plenty to order meals. Lucas chose the breakfast sampler while Alexander chose chocolate chip pancakes. The waiter returned with their coffee, and they placed their orders.

Preparing his coffee had become quite the ritual especially since he had anticipated it for so long and it marked the initiation of his greatest creation. Lucas poured a packet of cream into his cup and stirred the coffee slowly with a spoon. When the desired color change was complete, he put down the spoon and brought the cup to his nose. The fragrance brought him great joy, and the taste brought ecstasy. He closed his eyes to focus on the sensations.

Alexander, on the other hand, did not make much of a ritual out of his coffee, but he did go to great lengths to perfect the taste to his liking. He poured in three packets of cream and four packets of sweetener. Once the taste was palatable, he took a large gulp.

When Lucas opened his eyes, he found the aftermath of Alexander's flavoring. "What did you do?" he asked in horror at the scattered cream and sweetener packets and the dust of sweetener around his cup. "That's not how you drink coffee!"

"Taste pretty good to me." Alexander grinned and took another gulp.

Lucas prevented himself from making any further comment and contented himself with the focus of his own practice. Instead, he shifted the conversation. "I thought of something else about my flaws. I don't like how sometimes I act meanly to people, like insult them or act selfishly. Sometimes, I really do believe I'm better than someone and treat them poorly because of it. It's those flaws that scare me the most. They contradict my beliefs and make me feel like a hypocrite. They make me a hypocrite."

Alexander sipped his coffee and slowly placed the cup down. "It doesn't make you a hypocrite, man. It's a different thing entirely. Remember the lady who claimed that street as her own? You said she did that to get the love, acceptance, and community she needs. Whenever you act like that, I think you're doing the same thing. You're trying to fulfill your need for love acceptance, and community by misusing the social hierarchy. It's not the way you should go about it, but it doesn't mean you're a hypocrite. It makes you just as human as the rest of us. It means you, too, are struggling with the same dilemma.

"When you feel, you feel intensely, and when you hurt, you hurt greatly. In your pain, you desperately seek a way to stop it, but you don't know how to get the love you need because you haven't had the opportunity to learn how to create it. Your head understands the social hierarchy's influence on the love, acceptance, and community we receive, so it lashes out, hoping that putting someone else down will bring you love. But, this won't bring you love. Only your heart can solves this, and it does so with love. When you have no love directed your way, you must give what love you can to everyone, even if it feels like the end of you. Do this and you will create the love that keeps you alive. Only love keeps us going.

"These contradictions of self only happen when the head tries to do what only the heart can. This form of self-destruction happens when the head tries to simulate love, and every simulation ends horribly in one way or another. There are worse things you could have done. Be grateful you didn't go so far."

Lucas could not find the words to express his astonishment for the concept just presented and its source. Finally, he swallowed and managed "Dude, you have your moments. Incredible moments." His eyes remained wide, his eyebrows raised. With an effort, he forced himself to relax, blinking rapidly.

"Yup." Alexander smiled. "Whenever your head wants or tries to simulate love, no matter how harsh the means, you shouldn't attack yourself. You should ask yourself: 'Do I lack the love, acceptance, and community I need to get through the day? Have I loved anyone today?' Do that, and I guarantee those contradictions will decrease if not disappear entirely.

Lucas took a big sip of his coffee.

"Just remember, you're constantly doing the best you can to grow your heart and to love. I see it every day. There's no need for you to fear what you will do. There is only good inside you, man."

The waiter brought their food and sat their plates in front of them. As the aroma filled their nostrils, their mouths began to salivate with anticipation. Rich chocolatey pancakes towered under Alexander beckoning his knife and fork. Lucas gazed lovingly at the hash browns, bacon, ham, and eggs, then, at the two pancakes sliding into the clutter on another plate. Finally, a meal to start a worthy enterprise.

Lucas asked the waiter for Cholula and Alexander requested chocolate syrup. The waiter disappeared and reappeared with the condiments, and then, the glorious dressing began. The golden brown surface of the hash browns, the bright white of the eggs, and the redish brown of meat were all spotted with a vibrant orange. A viscous blackness slowly engulfed the great tower of chocolate pancakes until the plate almost ran over with syrup. With Alexander's permission, Lucas smothered his pancakes as well.

Slowly, with great care, Lucas cut his pancakes, eggs, and hash browns into bite size portions. As he stabbed a piece of pancake, a stillness overcame him. He stared at his plate, then spoke to Alexander. "We have been operating off an assumption that we have the capacity to be the very thing we need, but that's all it is. An assumption. An act of faith. Everything we've been talking about seems to have been one-sided, perhaps, even naïve. We've discussed the infinite possible expressions of beauty, but what of its opposite? What of the infinite possible expressions of the ugly? We can't overlook the fine line we walk between ultimate beauty, happiness, and boundless expression of our essence and extreme suffering, sorrow, and oppression. We are just as likely to destroy ourselves as we are to save ourselves."

Alexander stuffed his mouth with a four pancake thick forkful of chocolate. Chocolate syrup collected at the corners of his lips as he chewed mindfully, unshaken by Lucas' sudden pessimism. With his mouth still full, he responded. "Yup."

Incredulous, Lucas asked, "Yup? Don't you see this as a problem?"

Alexander licked the chocolate syrup from his lips and sipped his coffee. "Not at all, man. I thought that went without saying from the beginning. The way the world is now screams of the terrible things we are capable of and will always be capable of, but that doesn't have to get in the way of dreaming up a new world."

"Maybe not, but we do have to consider the possibility that we never will achieve a better world."

"Now, that's just nonsense! That's just as ridiculous as thinking the universe doesn't care about you. The universe doesn't care or not care about us. It exists beyond that kind of value system. Same with the progression of our world. Our world exists beyond any terms of evaluation like better. There's simply a direction of development that is optimal for our existence. Our world won't develop in ways that are right or wrong, good or bad. It can only develop into something that further facilitates our expression of our existence. Anything else isn't development."

"So, you're saying it's not a matter of achieving a better world. It's simply a matter of evolving or remaining stagnant."

"Exactly, and I don't see us ever becoming stuck forever. Yeah, we may have more 'dark ages', but if we still exist, we will continue to evolve. There's no avoiding it." Alexander shoved another forkful of pancake in his mouth.

"Well, can we say there are better evolutionary directions?"

Between chews, Alexander said, "Of course not. The only evaluation we could make is 'more optimal', but that's still iffy. Every path eventually leads to the same destination: infinitely more paths."

"That just puts us into an unsolvable riddle. There's no way to discern the best course of action. Instead, we have no choice but to grope in the dark and only hope we make it."

"And that's exactly the way it is and has always been and may always be. That's the nature of our existence."

"Then, how do I really do anything to help catalyze human evolution? How do I not feel powerless despite all the ideals I cling to?"

"Your power doesn't come from knowing the unknowable. It comes from actively manifesting the most optimal world you can with what is available for you to conceive. You may not know much, but as you develop, your knowledge will grow and you will be able to create an even more optimal world."

"I understand that, but what I find perplexing when I think about actively manifesting a new world is how I must act on nothing but faith and trust that though my perception is partial, it will provide enough for me to accomplish my dreams. I come face to face with ambiguity once again, but this time, I need to, at the very least, devise a methodology for navigating through this maze."

"What do you have in mind?"

Lucas' eyes fell to his plate. In his eyes, you could almost see the racing thoughts passing through his pin point focus. Still looking at his plate, Lucas took hold of his fork and began carefully skewering ham, egg, and hash brown. Then, he brought the fork to his mouth, closed his lips around it, and pulled the fork out, depositing the food on his tongue. He began chewing slowly.

Once he swallowed, he answered "Well, how does anyone

redesign our world? We need to identify a point of origin and the required skill sets to build from there. For starters, the person who successfully takes on this task will definitely need confidence in his or her perceptions not because they are accurate but because this person will know he or she has a piece of the puzzle."

"But, how does that inspire confidence?"

"Our perception is created from what the senses provide us, and our senses are tools we have evolved to interpret the universe around us. The origin of our perception is the universe itself, and because of this, our senses and the perceptions we construct from our senses, although partial, are born of the universe and are very real. Therefore, although our senses are limited to a small spectrum of existence, each and every one of us has a unique piece of the puzzle."

"So, no matter how incomplete our perception of the universe is, it is still something to stand on."

Lucas nodded. "Furthermore, this person will need to collect all the perceptions available in humanity and be able to combine them to create a collective human perception, which itself will be incomplete. Despite the incompleteness of our collective perception, however, this person would, hopefully, discover a quantifiable pattern to the linkage of individual perceptions to form the whole which could then be used to discern another quantifiable pattern to the linkage of the collective human perception to any other piece. What that is, I'm not sure. If there was another species as intelligent as humans, I would say that this collective perception is the next piece, but I suppose we will have to wait for another to reveal itself."

"And what exactly does this give this person? How will that help?"

"This would merely lay the intellectual foundation for everything to come. It's our person's point of departure. Like we've discovered there is no concrete point to build on; we need to construct a foundation for ourselves before we can design a new world."

"Yeah, but that doesn't solve the ambiguity problem. We still won't have certainty."

"You're absolutely right, but this only serves as a way to make sense out of the chaos, to try to clarify the ambiguity. Kind of like science, this won't truly explain anything, only describe it. We may not know how to get out of this maze, but we can map where we've been and predict what other parts will look like."

"Okay, so what else will this person need?"

"I think we covered what this person would need intellectually, though indirectly. So much goes into building a foundation like the one we described. Of primary importance is all the thought patterns that develop the person's ability to order the collective human perception and analyze its makeup. Just arriving at that point denotes a great deal of effort and an intricate understanding of the mind, but the intellect alone won't be enough."

"Oh, I agree, but why do you say so?"

"The intellect can only interpret information and calculate possible trajectories, but it cannot choose which trajectory we take. Yes, the intellect will amass the data we need to understand what a trajectory is and exactly its course, but it is the heart that must decide if the means and ends best suit us. The heart does not base its decision on logical assessments like 'more optimal' but on assessments of love, courage, and compassion. The heart decides which trajectory will fulfill our need for love, acceptance, and community not just from humans but all of existence as well. You can think of the heart as making its decisions based on a morality.

"Morality does not exist in the intellect. It resides in the heart. The intellect can only simulate morality, but this simulation will never survive the trials of life. Only the heart can manifest morality. The Morality of the Universe likewise, rest in the heart, and only through feeling it can we know it."

"Morality of the Universe?"

"Yes. When we think of morality, we think of a set of rules of right and wrong behaviors with other human beings. This is really the only context it is presented in, but morality encompasses much more than merely human to human interactions. Each species and every object is a part of a system that composes yet another system, and so on into infinity. The Morality of the Universe is what harmonizes all these parts and systems into a sustainable whole by guiding how each piece interacts with all other pieces."

"Wouldn't it be better to call it the Order of the Universe?"

"Perhaps, but I wish to avoid allowing the intellect a chance to dominate our perception. If I say order or law, it strays too closely to the scientific; becomes a construct of the intellect. I choose morality because no matter how hard the intellect may try, it will never enter the realm of the heart. To truly perceive morality, you must feel it, and this is exactly the aim of this part of our discussion. And, there is no relativity to it. The *feelings* are clear and consistent. What changes are our intellectualizations of them."

"I get it, man. This is an important point to make. I like that interpretation a lot better than rules we follow because we were told to. Yeah, man. That puts it in perspective." Alexander nodded fluidly, swaying his torso back and forth.

"But, the Intellect and the Heart are only tools we use to navigate our existence. We still need a direction, and that comes from us as well." Lucas paused.

"Man, you have to elaborate!"

Lucas smiled as he realized all had come full circle. "The evolutionary direction we seek does not need to be sought. Our existence naturally flows towards it, and what guides us, I call our Guiding Compass."

"Now, what do you mean by Guiding Compass?"

"Remember the night we met?" Alexander nodded. "That night something compelled me to go downtown. I felt it and thought it. I didn't need to consider it. My mind told me I needed to go, and my heart showered me with love and acceptance despite the oddity of it all. So, I went, and I met you. *That* is undoubtedly my Guiding Compass at work."

"Yeah, man! The same happened when I just knew someone would approach me, and when you did, it happened again. The unity of the head and the heart. It felt so natural."

"Exactly. In these moments, the Guiding Compass is easiest to perceive, but I normally find it not so easy. Being able to read the compass, if you will, is the last piece of awareness the person redesigning our world will need. Every aspect of the new world will *point* in the direction provided by the compass by facilitating our progress as individuals and as a species on our evolutionary trajectories.

"Our Redesigner will need the Head, Heart, and Guiding Compass working in tandem as the Triangle of Awareness. Only through this, can an optimal world be contrived and manifested to support our current form and facilitate our evolution."

"Wait," Alexander interjected. "I'm not sure how we could figure out what is optimal for our evolution. It's always been thought of as something random."

"Perhaps, but what if it isn't? I think it appears random because it doesn't conform to our expectations of a linear form, but this is a misperception on our part. I'm beginning to think the linearity of evolution is merely an illusion much like the illusionary linearity of time, and its randomness, not so random. I don't simply mean there are noticeable factors leading to an evolutionary change. Of course, there are, but knowing these factors does nothing to further our perception of the direction in which evolution flows.

"I'm saying that there is a form to evolution beyond this cross-sectional view; that infinite evolutionary outcomes already exist, and it is up to us which outcome we experience. We must become active agents of our own evolution; we must choose *how* we become. We must also design a world that best facilitates this by providing all our needs without hindering our growth and development."

"Okay." Alexander thought a moment. "Do we have any idea how this design will look like? I'm having trouble imaging it, but I like where we are going."

"Absolutely not, but I know it will have layers. Three important divisions will be the Micro, the Macro, and the Cosmic. The Micro will consist of individual human to human interactions."

"Like how we treat each other."

"Exactly. The Micro level makes up the fundamentals of our social world. Here we must maintain a nurturing disposition with all and ourselves. I don't think there is as much work to be done devising a plan for this level. After all, this has been our primary focus for the last few thousand years. We just need to truly implement our plan. Only if we support one another and solidify ourselves as the sturdiest of foundations, can we build a sustainable social or human world that reaches into the next level. The Macro."

"This must be society."

"Yes, but I want to specifically use the word civilization because it encompasses more than society. Society can too easily be misconstrued to only touch on interactions between groups of people, but the Macro includes not only this but how we interact with the planet as a whole."

Alexander smiled and threw his arms in the air. "Now you're talking!"

Lucas chuckled at the outburst. "This is the level we must really work on."

A look of disgust came over Alexander's face. "I'll say."

"An Optimal Civilizational Design must be created to ensure each individual has his or her needs met and is allowed to pursue their true expression of their existence and their very own evolutionary trajectory, while maintaining a harmonious relationship with the other species and natural processes of this planet. We must help support their current form and facilitate their evolution as well. The Earth, too, has its own expression we must respect and treat with love. We must allow all things, no matter how big or small, in existence to play their role in the universe, which brings us to the Cosmic level.

"Once we build the Macro level, we will likely push onward. Perhaps, this is truly our evolutionary trajectory, but we will never get to this point if we do not first build optimized Micro and Macro levels."

"You got that right!" Alexander chimed in. "If we don't, we will destroy ourselves first."

"At the Cosmic level, if we make it, we will begin building harmonious relationships with other planets, star systems, and galaxies and furthering our understanding of their roles in the universe. At this level, we would be foolish to attempt being more than observers. At least, with the limited experience and understanding we currently have. If we do make it to this point, I'm sure our role at this level will reveal itself. For now, I can only see us as the universe experiencing itself."

"Hey, man, this is a lot! A great starting point. I think the biggest issue the Redesigner would run into is resistance from humanity. We have to open people's minds before someone could really do this."

"That's why I want to write something we can use to help accomplish that. It will have to be people like us who open the doors for such an endeavor."

"Well, let's do it!"

Lucas fished his notebook and two pens from his backpack. When he sat back down, he tore out a few pages and handed them and a pen to Alexander. They cleared away their plates and leaned over their papers, pens scribbling away. The low hum of voices in the background seemed louder now in their silence.

Every few minutes, Lucas would stop, sip his coffee, gaze around, and then return to his work. Alexander also stopped often to drink his coffee, but in the intervals between Lucas' breaks such that it appeared as a tug-of-war for the creative energies coursing through the two. This dynamic continued for quite some time until Lucas disrupted the synchronicity by throwing down his pen and leaning back with a heavy sigh. He spotted their waiter, and after capturing his attention, requested more coffee.

After pouring himself another cup, Lucas went back to his writing, and immediately Alexander laid down his pen, sat back, and prepared himself a cup. As Alexander surveyed the restaurant, he noticed a dramatic increase in the number of customers packed into the surrounding tables and a rise in volume of the hubbub. Before him, his paper, with its black and white contrast, became a piercing photonic blade driving into his retinas. Alexander squeezed his eyes shut and rubbed them with his hands. Once the pain subsided, he forced himself back to work.

Lucas had drawn a concept map using circles connected by lines until his entire page appeared to emulate an amorphous molecular structure of disparate proportions. As he finished adding another circle with its proper connections, he dropped his pen, stood, and walked off to the restroom. When he returned, he found Alexander tapping his pen as he drank his coffee.

Alexander set down his cup and asked "Hey man, how's it going for you?"

"Not well." Lucas replied exasperatedly as he returned to his seat. "There's just so much. I'm not sure where to start or what all to include."

"Same here. I wrote this poem, but it's not really what I want."

"At least, you wrote something. So far, I just brainstormed."

"Well, what have you thought of so far?"

Lucas looked down at his paper and tapped it with his pen. "I haven't even started on the actual piece. I've just figured out what the piece must do, but I'm struggling to figure how it will do it." Lucas turned to a clean page in his notebook, and in the center, he drew a large circle. "This circle represents a person's inner most layer of or foundation for their psyche and their perception of reality."

Lucas, then, drew a dotted line surrounding the circle a few millimeters away. He drew another dotted line around the first, but this time shifted it so that the gaps of the first were covered by the solid sections of the second. "These dotted lines represent the barriers a person constructs to protect their perception from external influences, but these barriers are also the very thing preventing the person's growth. It's a confinement the person created for himself. As long as the person stays in this confinement, he will never become the change humanity needs."

Then, Lucas drew a line twisting and turning through the gaps of the dotted lines stopping at the edge of the inner circle. Next, he drew a line on both sides of the tip to indicate an arrow head pointing to the circle. "This line represents what our piece must do. We must create something that bypasses the barriers through their gaps and holes to reach the person's core, however, here is the most difficult part. We must create something that readily absorbs into their core on their own. Whatever we create must flow naturally into the person like a hormone into a cell. We cannot penetrate their core because that will only hurt them and completely undermine our efforts. So, I'm still trying to figure out what we must use to get through to people."

"The only thing I can think of is love, but that will only get through their barriers and seep into their core. It doesn't deliver a message. Maybe, there's a way to package a message in love, so the message reaches their core."

"Perhaps, or should we create something that inspires them to lower their walls without trying to deliver a message? Something that showers them with love, acceptance, and community. Perhaps, with their walls down, they will naturally grow to see what we see."

Alexander nodded. "Maybe, but I know ideas by themselves will do nothing. People's barriers are too guarded against ideas, which makes sense. The only reason these barriers exist is because people are afraid, and most likely of losing their love, acceptance, and community, and having ideas different from what we are conditioned to have will definitely threaten how much we receive. The barriers are just a product of our conditioning, and they confine us to what we think will give us the love we need." Alexander shook his head. "I don't know, man."

"Yeah, me neither." Lucas brought his concept map back in front of him. "I'm going to get back at it."

Alexander went out front to smoke a cigarette while Lucas dived deep into his thoughts. Lucas figured pacing would help churn out his thoughts, so he stood and paced near their table in an area that minimized his obstruction of others passing by. As he paced back and forth he carried his notebook and pointed to various circles with his pen mumbling to himself. Other customers began casting inquiring glances his direction.

When Alexander returned, he smiled in amusement at the spectacle before him. Lucas reminded him of a great artist on the verge of birthing his masterpiece. With each step, determination seemed to grow exponentially in Lucas' countenance. *We* both *will do this*. Alexander sat down and with revitalized enthusiasm, began writing.

A few minutes later, their waiter approached. "Hey guys, sorry to interrupt. The restaurant is getting very busy. Do you mind paying and leaving? You've been here for quite a while."

Lucas looked up from his notebook in dismay. "Are you sure we can't stay longer? We are working on something very important. We're trying to create a catalyst for humanity to break free from its millennia long cycle of tragedy."

"I'm sorry, but my manager request you leave. We need the table space."

Alexander pleaded "Come on, man! We've been waiting for this moment for days."

"No," Lucas interrupted, "we will go. I understand you have a business to run."

Frustrated and disheartened, Alexander and Lucas gathered their things and proceeded to the cash register at the front. Lucas handed over the payment and a decent tip for the waiter despite their forced premature departure. After concluding the transaction, they exited the IHOP.

They walked back to the field where they slept and where they hoped to find comfort amongst the trees. After laying down their things, they climbed the same tree Lucas tried to fuse his consciousness to. A gentle but firm breeze coaxed them from their disappointment.

Lucas broke the silence. "What do we do now?"

"We can continue writing here. I like the vibes of the place."

With a touch of sadness Lucas replied, "I don't know if I can right now or at all for that matter. When I try to sequence my thoughts to create an intelligible formation of words, my mind shuts down, and a fog completely consumes me. I know I need to, at least, take a break."

"Yeah, man. You describe it perfectly." Alexander stared off in thought. "Alright, I got it. We can head back downtown near my house and that bar. They probably have a band playing tonight. Maybe, we could check it out. I think we need to have some fun."

"I like that idea. We can try to write again later."

They climbed down the tree, picked up their things, and Alexander led them to the bus stop across the street. About an hour and a few snack bars later, a bus pulled up, and they boarded. This bus driver, too, paid little attention to the two, and again, they managed to ride without paying. The ride was a long one, but the time flew by, especially when a fellow passenger asked them to play. Everyone enjoyed the break from monotony, including the driver. Some even handed them cash in appreciation. Their spirits began to rise.

Once they arrived downtown, the sun disappeared behind the skyscrapers, but its dim glow still reached from the horizon. The walk from the terminal to the bar taxed their legs, but once it came into view, a new vigor overcame them. A crowd gathered out front killing the time before the band performed by drinking beer and socializing. Tables were placed outside and filled. Those who could not sit, stood. The place gleamed with life.

Alexander found a place for their things out of the way but still in view, and led them into the group. A figure of extravagant fashion guarded the door collecting the admission fee from each eager individual. Alexander approached the man to inquire the necessity of payment in the hopes of a lucky break of benevolence, however, the man did not waver in his resolve. After assessing their assets, they discovered a deficit too great for either to enter.

Fortunately, the sentry permitted Lucas and Alexander to enjoy themselves outside where they could sit at a table and listen to the muffled sounds, as well as converse with the people congregating out front. Alexander determined himself to take full advantage of this opportunity. If he could not enter the bar, then he would create his own environment on its border.

They sat on a small staircase near their bags to wait for the mass of people to clear from the front and free a table for them. As they waited, Alexander lit himself a cigarette, and Lucas leaned against the door at the top of the stairs. Lucas looked to the dim dots above him striving to shine through the smog but with a brilliance barely visible. Those stars suffered the same fate as he did. No matter how hard he tried, he still could not achieve the brilliance he knew he was capable of, but he found solace in realizing like the stars above him, he, too, burned bright.

Lucas turned to Alexander. "You know I go home tomorrow, right?"

"Yeah, man. The journey's almost over. That's why tonight is so important. We need to make the most of it."

"I agree. Tonight, we have to make an impact no matter how slight. We have to do it for all the stars trying to shine through the smog above us."

Alexander smiled, leaned back, and inhaled deeply through his cigarette. His chin pointed as he thought over Lucas' words. Something in Lucas finally clicked. What exactly, Alexander could not tell, but here was Lucas speaking in his language. *What a remarkable statement!* Lucas had grown; Alexander had no doubt about it.

The mass of people began filing into the bar like a slow but forceful stream. Slowly, the numbers shrank until only a few remained scattered about the patio. Their moment of opportunity arrived, so Lucas and Alexander grabbed their instruments and hurried to an available table.

They sat watching more passersby in search of entertainment file into the bar after discovering the live music within. Muffled melodies permeated the façade along with blasts of decibels whenever the door opened. Conversation remained minimal save the occasional small talk from curious eyes that had befallen the two. Lucas focused his attention on the architecture of the social edifice before him. If he could understand its design and how it held itself together, perhaps, he could find his way in.

A man with a large smile stood expectantly at the edge of their table. His eyes fixed on their instruments. "You guys play?"

"Sure do." Lucas responded before Alexander had a chance.

"You should play. So what if there's a show inside; no reason you can't play out here."

"You make an excellent point!" Lucas agreed. "We shall, indeed." He looked to Alexander afraid he was too hasty and inconsiderate in his decision, but Alexander simply readied his guitar and began playing. Lucas joined in as soon as the melody got underway.

The man took a seat at one of the open chairs at their table and listened with a smile. Every now and then, he sipped his beer as he bobbed his head to their music. Others sitting or standing nearby turned towards the two, watching with approval. Certainly, this was a fitting addition to the festivities of the night. The doorman also glanced every now and again at Lucas and Alexander between his collections. He, too, seemed to approve. Once their curiosities were satisfied, those looking on returned to their conversations or drinking their beer in peace.

The first song ended, and immediately, Alexander began another from the four he knew. Lucas flowed along. More people gathered on the patio, taking breaks from the loudness within or moving to an environment more conducive to conversation. Many couples were about, usually a man and a woman hovering close to each other. As they moved, they moved as one, and as they spoke, they spoke as one. Lucas watched them as he played, noting how their proximity and unison were only partially engineered by them but completed by the rest.

Lucas looked at the many other faces laughing, smiling, and chatting away. He saw eye contact made by one and held or averted by the other. People lounged in chairs smoking cigarettes and nodding as another spoke. An effervescent few shined while others seemed to hide yet moved closer to the illumination.

Lucas' gaze returned to the doorman and his appealing dress. The doorman wore black and gray suede oxfords, black dress pants, a black dress shirt with a gray vest covered in vertical, black stripes, and a gray fedora with a black band circling the top. A feather stuck out of the band on the left side. He sat alone at a table higher and smaller than the rest smoking a black cigarette.

When the song ended, Lucas put down his drum and excused himself from the table. Alexander said "Go for it, man" and proceeded to light himself another cigarette. As Lucas walked away, he heard the man strike up conversation with Alexander. "That's a nice guitar you have there."

Lucas strode up to the doorman's table and struck up a conversation of his own. "Hey man, how's it going?"

The doorman smiled a smile that reached his eyes, and in that smile, Lucas felt a great warmth. "It's going pretty well, my friend. How about you?"

Lucas felt something in this man or rather emanating from him. Lucas began tripping over his thoughts forgetting why he had come, but then, that warmth seeped into him, soothing his anxiety and placing the ground beneath his feet. After a breath, Lucas replied "Been an interesting ride lately, but it's going well. Do you mind if I join you?"

"Not at all." The doorman gestured to the only other chair at the table. "Take a seat."

"Thanks." Lucas hoisted himself upon the tall chair. "I really like your outfit. Great style."

"Thank you." The doorman gave that warm smile again.

"It looks fantastic. Do you by any chance know what you are trying to emulate by dressing so?"

The man looked thoughtfully at Lucas, eyebrows slightly raised as he mulled over the enquiry. "That's a good question. I'm not sure I do, but I don't think I know exactly what you mean."

"Well, everything we say or do are constructs we build upon our foundation or better yet, our perception of reality, so everything must emulate something of our perception of reality, be it values, ideas, or a direction. I can't be any more specific, or I run the risk of answering my own question."

The doorman chuckled. "Alright then. I don't think I considered more than that I like it. It fits my vision of me. I feel good wearing this." The man took another drag of his black cigarette. "What about you?"

Lucas was taken by surprise. He didn't think of the possibility that his question would be redirected at him. He rarely did. "Now, this will be difficult. Give me a moment to think, please." Lucas examined himself, starting with his feet and moving to his shoulders. He wore brown leather desert boots with a high back covering his ankle. The edge of his black socks protruded a half inch above the back of the shoe. His shins lay bare until they met the gaudy, beige, plaid shorts just under his knees. Dark stains of dirt he acquired when climbing the tree earlier that day streaked across his thighs.

He kept his eyes moving and discovered he had on a green shirt a little too baggy for his taste with big, bright, white letters spelling *IRISH* across his chest. He would never wear an outfit of this sort to an establishment such as this. He noticed that dirt speckled his legs and arms, and for the first time he smelled the consequence of not showering for a few days. His breath, too, he surmised must smell something awful, and his hair, certainly, must have a greasy look. Lucas had completely forgotten what he wore and the state of his hygiene. Suddenly overcome, he looked abashed, but quickly regained his composure.

"I wear my journey. These past few days I have been staying on the streets with my friend." He pointed to Alexander. "I brought these clothes because I didn't care what happened to them, but they have come to mean much more. Perhaps before my journey, they held a different meaning, but now, they represent a struggle for an impossible metamorphosis." Lucas made eye contact with the doorman; his passion bursting from his sockets.

The doorman met Lucas' eyes and smiled. "Now, that is a very intriguing answer. You must tell me more of this journey."

As Lucas began to speak, another man in a black t-shirt and dark blue jeans approached from behind. He stood next to the doorman with his arms crossed, surveying the crowded patio while he asked "How's everything out here?" Lucas saw the man's gaze stop when it reached their equipment and then moved on.

The doorman replied in a familiar but respectful tone "Everything's good out here, boss."

"Good, we have a big crowd tonight. Be sure you're collecting admission from everyone, and be on the lookout for those homeless kids that hang around here. I don't want them disturbing anyone. They already started leaving their bags over there." He said the last sentence with disgust.

"Actually," Lucas interrupted, "that's my friend's and my stuff."

The boss looked incredulously at Lucas. "Why do you have bags packed like that?"

"I'm staying on the streets with my friend to see what it's like to be homeless."

The boss stared at Lucas for a moment. "That's stupid. Really stupid." As Lucas began explaining himself, the boss cut him off saying to the doorman "Let me know if trouble starts." Then, he turned and went back into the bar. Lucas watched him walk away with his mouth still open.

The doorman gave Lucas a compassionate look. "I'm sorry he did that. Please, tell me about your journey."

Lucas struggled to recover from the unexpected blow. "I…I…

Yes, I'm staying on the streets with my friend." His voice wavered in and out of the hubbub. "I'm searching for an answer, no a solution, for my pain. I'm trying to work myself into the core of everything that is wrong. I'm trying to make a change." His eyes now seemed to retreat inside him.

"What have you found?"

"I found…" The statement died away. Lucas looked around, saw the people still smiling, laughing, and chatting. He saw a couple kissing at a table to themselves. He closed his eyes.

A group of four women approached the table offering greetings to the doorman. The doorman returned their greeting and added "You all look lovely tonight." They smiled and blushed and thanked him. Then, he informed them of the admission fee and collected their payments. After the women passed to go inside, the doorman returned his attention to Lucas, waiting expectantly.

Lucas opened his eyes and turned to the doorman. "I found more questions. Better questions, but only questions. I want to say I found nothing, but I can't discount all I have learned to arrive here, in this bigger mystery."

The doorman smiled widely. "Now, that sounds exactly like one of my songs. Cheer up friend. You've made it through quite a distance. Keep moving forward and never give up."

Lucas smiled a strained smile, but really did feel lifted. "Thank you. If you don't mind, I want to return to my friend."

"Not at all. I'll be here if you want to continue talking."

Lucas slid out of the chair and walked back to the table where Alexander sat. The man he left there still engrossed himself in conversation with Alexander.

"That really is a nice guitar. How'd you come by it?" The man said.

"Thanks, man. My friend gave it to me about a week ago. He said it would serve a better purpose in my hands and then gave it to me."

"Wow, that's a great friend! I'm glad your friend did that because he was right. You play pretty well. I play a little myself, you know. I have a beautiful acoustic at home."

"I bet." Alexander held his guitar to the man. "Want to play?"

"Well, now the drummer is back. You guys should play."

"Sure thing, man." Alexander began a blues song, and Lucas joined in happy to be at that table again with his djembe and

Alexander. More people gathered around to watch, but one woman determined herself to do more than merely spectate. She pulled up a chair to Lucas and asked his permission to play on one half of his djembe. Lucas smiled and still playing, shifted in his seat, so his djembe pointed towards her.

Lucas kept the skeleton beat to allow the woman the opportunity to flow freely with the music in a broader range of expression. She knew what she was doing. A little better than Lucas in fact. Her accents filled in nicely and in ways Lucas could not manage himself. She would join him in the skeleton, then venture off here and there, but always returning and always on time. Lucas admired her.

Alexander lost himself in the new energy the woman brought and could not rid the grin from his face. He strummed passionately and sang loudly as onlookers clapped along. This was by far the best he ever played. He was uncertain what he felt, but whatever it was, it felt better than anything in years.

When the song ended, the three musicians laughed together, and the small crowd cheered. Lucas complimented the woman and said how glad he was she joined. "You're not so bad yourself," she replied, and something fluttered within him. Then, the man who inspired the session stood and announced "I'm buying you guys beers. What do you drink?"

"Whatever you drink is good for me," answered Alexander. The man turned to Lucas. "Same here." Then, he turned to the women. "Whatever you like." She smiled. The man smiled and nodded, then headed towards the bar.

Alexander called after him. "Hey, man. Make sure you buy yourself one, so we can drink together."

The man turned around. "Of course!" He smiled again, then went inside.

Alexander lit another cigarette he acquired from the man and leaned back in his chair, looking to the stars. He closed his eyes and inhaled deeply. Lucas looked at the woman still sitting next to him and showing no sign she would leave anytime soon. He took a moment to appreciate the beauty before him. She wore bright blue pants and brown sandals. Her shirt a vibrant white. The outfit stood out strikingly against her light brown skin, black hair, and dark brown eyes.

Suddenly, she turned to Lucas, and he quickly looked away.

143

"Where did you get your djembe? It's a great drum."

Lucas exclaimed "You know its name! That's great! Not many do. People keep calling it a bongo or bongo*s.*" Lucas laughed and shook his head. "I found it at a flea market in New Orleans."

"Lucky find." She reached over to touch the wood and feel its carvings. "So, are you out trying to make money with your friend?"

"What?" Lucas looked puzzled.

"You and your friend look a bit shabby, and I guessed those are your bags over there." She pointed to their equipment. "Sorry, if I assumed wrongly. I didn't mean any offense."

Lucas shook himself from his surprised. "No offense taken. You're right. That is our stuff. I didn't realize it was so obvious, but I'm not trying to make money tonight."

The man returned with four beer bottles, two in each hand. "Here we are!" He handed out the beers, then took his seat across from Alexander. He raised his bottle in a toast, and the others followed suit. "To wonderful music and the great people who play it!" The man went down the line lightly tapping his bottle with each of theirs. Lucas smirked at Alexander as their bottles touched. "Cheers!" Then, they both clinked their bottles with the woman's. Alexander continued talking to the man while Lucas addressed the woman.

"I'm not really homeless by the way. I'm just staying a few days on the streets with my friend to see what homelessness is like and to see what else I can learn. He's actually homeless, though." He finished with a hint of sadness in his voice.

Now, she appeared surprised, but nodded for him to continue when she saw him open his mouth to speak further.

"Did you know there's a street not too far from here that has its sidewalks covered with sleeping people every night?"

"No, I didn't." Her mouth curved into a frown. "That's terrible!"

"Sure is, and I can't think of anything responsible except the social hierarchy and our adherence to it which has to be the most ridiculous reason."

She nodded. "I agree it's ridiculous. I'm from Honduras, and it's worse there. You can see the inequality everywhere you go. You have nice, large houses next to homes too small for the family living in it, and some are falling apart."

"That's awful! I want to do something about it! I can't stand just seeing ridiculous and unnecessary suffering and not doing something about it."

"What would you do?" She asked intrigued.

Out of nowhere, the boss appeared in front of their table staring sternly at Alexander. "Do you have an ID?"

Alexander tried to keep his composure and usual smoothness but still sounded apologetic. "No sir, I…"

Rage shot from the boss' eyes as he reached forward and ripped the beer bottle out of Alexander's hand. He went to Lucas and tore his bottle away as well. Then, he yelled "You dare drink without an ID at *my bar*!" The boss stomped to a trashcan and threw the bottles into it with a clash and the sound of glass breaking.

Lucas reacted before he could stop himself. "Hey man, I have my ID!"

The boss glared contemptuously at him a moment, then yelled "Get out of here!" Lucas and Alexander were too shocked to move. "Now!" With that last impetus, they rose from their chairs and slowly walked to their equipment. They avoided the eyes of the onlookers, especially the boss'. Before they left, Lucas waved to the woman. She waved back with a sad look on her face.

"I don't want to see you back here, you hear?"

Alexander led them away, ignoring the boss as he yelled after them. They walked in silence towards Alexander's home. They did not discuss where they would go. They did not need to. There was no other decision to make. A couple of times, Alexander tried to break the silence, but he, too, let his attempts fail. When they reached the parking lot, Alexander weaved through the cars in his usual manner, however, his serpentine path lost much of its curvature. Lucas walked a straight line.

After making their way through the fences, sliding one section open and shut and climbing over another, Lucas stopped to stare at the large sloping wall in front of him. Alexander climbed the steps on the wall and threw down the rope they had left at the top. Lucas grabbed hold of the rope and began pulling himself up, leaving their equipment behind. One hand moving in front of the other, pulling as a foot rose further up the wall. Then, again with the other hand and foot.

Once he scaled five feet, he paused as if contemplating his next step. Suddenly, he let go of the rope as he kicked off the wall and pulled his knees to his head, flipping backwards. He landed in a semi squat and quickly straightened himself. Alexander stared at him with wide eyes.

"No!" Lucas roared. A bird on the opposite side of the underbelly darted from its hiding place and flew away. "I will not let *this night* end *this way*!" Tears streaked down his cheeks as he stood staring at that vertical slab of concrete before him.

Instinctively, Alexander moved closer to the hanging strand of rope. He stopped himself and tried to console Lucas. "Hey man, forget that guy. He's lost his way from beauty. Things like that happen all the time. You just have to keep moving."

Lucas gazed imploringly at Alexander. "How can I just forget what happened? That man is a human being, and he is actively, before my very eyes, creating a terrible world! How do I just go to sleep after I just realized how everything that hurts us; destroys us is manifested? And, all those people just watched. Even, the woman. I thought she was different, something beautiful, but she's as bad as the rest of them."

Alexander could not find the words to help Lucas, so instead, he sat on the ledge and listened as Lucas paced back and forth.

"They could have stopped him. Yes, I know you not having an ID is illegal, but how you handle these situations is vital to the creation of a proper micro level. You can't just start attacking! Where was the love that would actually make a change? And, all these people. They are the ones responsible for ensuring the world we create is one of love and beauty. We all are!

"But, they just sat there as though they were powerless and not depended on. I just saw humanity use its own hand to destroy itself! We will never rise from the mud this way! Someone has to return their autonomy of their perception of reality and wake them from their learned helplessness. I'm not sure this person is me! If not me, then who? Will you Alexander? Please, you have to!"

Lucas fell to his knees not caring for the dirt, weeping. Alexander sat on the ledge baffled and clueless what to do except watch and listen and be there with Lucas. Face in hands, Lucas spoke through tears, but Alexander could not understand his muffled words. "Hey man, what was that?"

Lucas dropped his hands and yelled "If we can't handle such a simple social situation, how could we ever redesign civilization? I don't know if I can do this. I can't do this!" Lucas dropped his face back into his hands and wept harder.

Alexander grabbed the rope and walked down the wall. He knelt next to Lucas, putting his arm around his shoulders as he said "Hey man, I need you to hang in there. I *need* you to. You've brought so much light to my life in so little time. *We* will try together. It doesn't matter if we succeed or fail. It's the struggle that's important. As long as we struggle to grow, learn, and love, we are fulfilling our roles in existence. We make the universe proud, man."

Lucas' weeping lessened. "You're right, but I didn't know it would be so hard to watch people destroy themselves." He remained there staring at the large slopping wall before him.

Alexander began gathering their things and taking them to his home. Lucas watched as Alexander climbed up and then down and up and down again. At the end of his last trip, Alexander picked up Lucas' backpack and the laptop bag still bulging with the water jug, but as he passed Lucas, a hand reached out to stop him. Lucas clung fiercely to his backpack, so Alexander set it down beside him. Then, Alexander began climbing the rope. Once he reached the top, he laid the laptop bag down and made their pallet carefully placing their pillows where their heads would lay. He did not need to console Lucas any longer. He knew Lucas would need this time to feel and grow.

Sometime later, Lucas maneuvered his legs from beneath him and stood. He threw on his backpack and walked to the far right end of the wall where the steps protruded. Driven by impulse and nothing more, Lucas ran up the wall and took hold of the first step. He strained to pull himself on top the step under the weight of his bag but managed to maintain an air of ease. Then, the next step he conquered much the same way by jumping up and hoisting himself onto its flat surface.

Lucas only stopped a moment to feel the breeze lightly stroke through his hair and bring life to his limbs. Suddenly, he darted forward to leap, but something hindered the full potential of his legs. When he kicked off the wall between the steps, he knew he would not make it. He knew he would fall short, and if he did not grab hold of the step with whichever part of his body did reach it, he would fall to the cement below.

His arms moved quickly on their own accord. Reactions. Involuntary survival mechanisms to protect oneself from oneself.

No, it was not his will that saved him, at least not his conscious will, but perhaps, the will inherent in all manifestations of existence to exist. That ethereal, ineffable force that tells us to persevere when we have entirely forsaken ourselves. That consciousness that usurps our own and commands our bodies, despite our protests, to keep us alive when we no longer care to live. Something would not allow Lucas to hurt himself, but it was not Lucas.

The edge of the concrete protrusion collided with his chest causing a slight constriction of his rib cage and a painful disturbance of the organs within. The air abandoned his lungs. His fingertips clenched the grooves of the flat surface of the step as the skin of his arms gripped the rough concrete in a desperate attempt to keep the rest of him from falling. Lucas dangled there in awe and contemplation. He smiled.

I could just let go. It's that easy. Just have to fall right. Head first.

Alexander ran to the ledge in a panic. "You alright, man? I'll grab the rope!" Then, he dashed for the rope.

Lucas still smiled, but shortly, his smile faded into consternation as his arms and shoulders and back contracted. Slowly, he started to rise onto the step. *Why? Why keep going?* Now, his abdomen lay on the surface, and still, his body crept slowly up. Lucas tried to undo the progress by commanding his arms to push instead of pull, but they did not listen. Once his legs slid over the edge and his struggle completed, he knelt staring at the ground below. *You are not finished yet.* Lucas clamped his eyes shut, tilted his head back, and released a broken, weepy, bestial howl.

Alexander watched Lucas from the ledge above concerned and perplexed. He let the rope fall to Lucas' side. For five minutes, he stood there observing, waiting, but then, he returned to their pallet to lay watching the dancing lights above him. After a long while, Lucas climbed up the wall, placed his backpack against a column, put away the rope, and laid on his half of their pallet. Shortly, they both drifted off to sleep.

DAY FOUR

There was only the burning somewhere, yet everywhere. *What are you?* He tried to investigate, but this feeling was the only stimulus available for him to perceive. It felt like fire. *Stop it! Why are you doing this to me?* The burning grew in intensity; the pain pulsated through him, until Lucas shot up from where he lay. He searched desperately for the source, and on his left forearm, he found a fire ant clinging to him. He wiped the ant away and rubbed his arm vigorously.

The gray of predawn bathed everything in a dull hue. A cool breeze ruffled leaves and sent branches swaying. Birds warmed up for the daily singing, and slowly, life awakened all around. The rumble of an engine sounded in the distance as a car drove along the road that met perpendicularly to the bridge. Waves danced across the surface of the bayou. Lucas rose from the pallet.

He stretched, spreading his arms as wide as possible and then rotated his arms and shoulders. He squatted as low as he could and then stood slowly, letting the tension enter and leave his legs. He rubbed his arm where the ant had bit him as he examined Alexander still wrapped in his blanket and sound asleep. Lucas walked over to the ledge of relief and relieved himself. No one was around, but he no longer cared. The sun reached over the horizon as he stood watching a stream of urine fall and splatter on the ground below.

Once finished, Lucas walked back to the pallet but stopped ten feet away. A smile slowly, slowly grew at the corner of his mouth as he gazed at Alexander's home. He noticed the wrinkles of the sheets and blankets on which they slept and the dirt on their edges. He shifted his attention to their back packs, his sitting on top a pile of small rope and Alexander's by his feet where he lay. Then, Lucas stared at Alexander's guitar resting on the ground next to him. Alexander stirred in his sleep, kicking off his blanket and then settling down again. Graffiti covered the wall blocking the ledge adjacent to their pallet.

Lucas opened his backpack and fished out his phone from underneath his dirty clothes and the equipment he never used. He laughed quietly. *I wonder how much easier it would have been if I didn't have all this excess weight.* He turned his phone on and moved back to where he stood in observation. He captured a picture of the scene. *I will want to keep this for a long time to come.*

He walked to the ledge of the large sloping wall they had climbed the night before and sat with his feet dangling off the side. He messaged his father, informing him of his reluctant readiness to come home. As he waited for a reply, he leaned back on his hands and watched the world go by. Every few minutes, a car passed slowly, without haste. People, now, crossed the bridge above, projecting their voices and laughter. The breeze still blew strong, caressing him and bringing movement to the static environment. Squirrels ran across the park and up the trees. His phone vibrated. The message read "Now?" Lucas sent confirmation and then slid his phone into his pocket.

He returned to enjoying the peace and the subdued bustle of others. Someone in the parking lot exclaimed to her friends "There's somebody up there!" Lucas, however, just sat there in his silence, paying no heed until he heard Alexander rise.

"Good morning, man." Alexander still appeared concerned for Lucas.

"Good morning."

Alexander stood and walked to the designated ledge to relieve himself. He wore no shirt, just bright red shorts and his bandana. When he returned, Lucas, still staring at the world, said "I leave today, but I don't want to. I feel the emptiness of my *normal* life more than ever, now."

"You can always stay on the streets with me." Alexander grinned, and Lucas laughed.

"That's not my role. I'm just a traveler of realities, and my journey is nowhere near finished. There are more perceptions of reality to explore, but first I have to return to my dad's house." Lucas reached over for his backpack and dug for his wallet. He counted the remaining money within. "Are you hungry? We are about six dollars short to buy two sandwiches from Subway. There's one three blocks up the road. We can play to make the rest."

"Yeah, man. I'm starving! We're good on cash, though. The guy who bought us beers gave me a ten." Alexander walked to his pants and pulled out the ten dollar bill.

Lucas stood to begin packing, and after Alexander changed, he started packing as well. They laid out their queen sized blankets, folded them in half lengthwise, and then rolled them into a tight cylinder. Next, they laid their sheets out and folded them in half and rolled the cylinders inside the sheets. Then, they placed their pillows on top and tied twine around all to secure the bundle.

They collected whatever they had taken or had fallen out of their backpacks and stuffed them inside. Once everything was packed, they tied their bundles as far to the top of their bags as possible. Then, they slid their clubs through the openings in the rope, between bag and bundle. Lastly, they attached their water bottles.

Alexander threw down the rope while Lucas threw on his backpack and grabbed his djembe and then gathered his things. Alexander descended first, but before Lucas followed, he took one more long look around. When Lucas reached the ground, he tossed the rope up and over the ledge above. Then, they proceeded to climb over the first fence section and opened the other. With a loud clang, Lucas closed the sliding section. Slowly, he removed his hand.

The first crunch of grass beneath their feet came as a comfort, and with each step, purpose swelled within them. Alexander quickened his pace, and Lucas raised his head. Not as many cars occupied the parking lot but enough for them, both, to weave their serpentine paths. Lucas made an effort to eliminate any trace of linearity as he twisted and turned. As they stepped foot on the sidewalk, a train passed on their left, stopping traffic, so they cross the street without worry.

Not many people roamed the streets, but some passed by, walking calmly, without rush. The bars were closed and deserted. Lucas looked sullenly at the patio where last night's scene occurred, but they did not linger. At the next intersection, they crossed to their left, and then, crossed right, returning to their original heading on the opposite side of the street. On the corner of the last intersection stood the Subway with its "OPEN" sign flashing. Alexander pulled open the glass door, and they entered.

A woman was the sole customer ahead of them in line and in the establishment. Lucas and Alexander waited as she instructed the woman behind the counter how to prepare her sandwich. Another woman appeared from the back and walked to where Lucas and Alexander stood. "What can I get for you today?" Both ordered the exact same as before, a meatball marinara sandwich for Lucas and a vegetarian sandwich for Alexander.

The customer before them still moved along from topping to topping, but the woman serving Lucas and Alexander moved so fast that she filled their orders at approximately the same time as her counterpart finished the other customer's. All the sandwiches were wrapped one after another and clustered near the cash register. The woman before them paid, grabbed her cup, and walked out of the way. Lucas and Alexander, then, paid and received their cups from the smiling woman across the counter. "Enjoy your meal."

They thanked her and went to the soda fountain. Lucas made no hesitation in selecting Root Beer, his favorite. Alexander filled his cup with Coke. Once they secured their lids and inserted their straws, they sat at a table adjacent to one of many large windows. As they unwrapped their sandwiches, Lucas discovered he was given the wrong sandwich, and the meat on it indicated it was not Alexander's either. "I think they gave me that women's sandwich." He rewrapped the sandwich and strode over to where the woman sat. She had not yet unwrapped the one she was given.

"Excuse me, but the lady must have mixed up our sandwiches. I believe I have yours."

She frowned as Lucas revealed part of her sandwich. "Oh, no!" He gestured for them to exchange, and she frowned again. "Okay, but you're not dirty are you?" She looked at his clothes and oily hair. "I mean you didn't get my sandwich dirty did you?"

Lucas sighed and shook his head. "Of course not."

"Well, alright then." She accepted her sandwich from Lucas and handed him his. "Thank you."

"Not a problem" he replied and then walked away to their table. Alexander had already started devouring his sandwich. Lucas sat and did the same. The steam rising from the marinara sauce and meatballs made his eyes water as he took a bite. One thing he knew for sure, no matter how bad things became, food would always be a wonderful delight amidst the most tempestuous of times. He savored the welcomed titillation of his taste buds.

They did not speak until they both finished their meals and sipped on their sodas. Then, Lucas broke the silence. "I didn't write anything. I feel disappointed with myself."

"Hey, man that doesn't matter." Alexander waved away the notion. "What happened was what was meant to happen. You may not have written anything, but man, you've grown since we started. That's what's important, bro. I don't think you were here to write anything this time. I think you were here to learn and wake me up." Alexander chuckled. "I haven't thought so hard and so much ever. I'm exhausted, man, but I love it!"

"Perhaps, but I don't feel content. I still feel like there's a task left undone, and I can't rest before I complete it, no matter how hard the struggle or how much I suffer."

"Of course, you do!" Alexander smiled. "You have a lot to do, and me too. Humanity needs us, and the universe calls out to us. We have a world to change, *together*, man."

Lucas smiled and took another sip of his drink. "I hope, for my sake, you're right. I can't ever go back to how I was living, before this. I just can't."

"Then, don't! You have a choice, man. You always do, and you're always welcome to join me."

Lucas laughed. "You know, I probably will be going on another journey with you. Perhaps, we will walk across the U.S. together."

"Yeah, man. I'm totally down for that."

Lucas locked eyes with Alexander. "Take good care of yourself, man. I need you in my life."

"Oh, I will." Alexander grinned. "You don't have to worry about me."

"I have nothing, now, but someday I will, and when that day comes, you're welcome to join me. You will always have a safe place with me, when I get my place. I'll help you get off the streets and really get things together, if you are still out here. I want you to truly pursue your dreams. You are important to me."

Alexander smiled at Lucas. "You don't have to worry about me. I'll manage. I tell you what. When I get my own place, you can come stay with me!"

They laughed together. Once Lucas caught his breath he said "My dad will pick me up around noon. We still have a bit of time to kill. Want to go play outside?"

"Absolutely!"

They gathered their things, threw away their empty cups and wrappings, and exited through the glass door. Lucas did not want to walk far. In fact, Lucas did not want to walk further than five feet from the entrance, so they placed their equipment on the sidewalk to sit on. As Alexander warmed up his fingers, Lucas opened the laptop bag and removed the empty jug. Then he laid the bag open in front of them for ritual's sake and then positioned his djembe between his knees. They began to play.

No one passed near them. Some walked on the opposite side of the street, but they paid the two no attention, seemingly deaf to the music. Another train passed on their left, picking up and dropping off those few passengers. The lack of an audience, however, was of no importance. They played not for others nor material gain. They played for the universe.

Two men on bicycles rounded the corner and rode up as Alexander and Lucas finished the song they played. One man looked middle aged and weathered by a hard life. The other appeared only a few years older than them. Lucas and Alexander stared questioningly as the older man dismounted.

The older man asked with genuine concern "Have you guys eaten today?"

"Actually, we just ate," Alexander replied. "Thanks, though."

The man reached into his pocket and pulled out a large stack of gift cards for various restaurants and fast food chains. "You sure? I'm given these to feed the homeless, so you don't have to worry about taking money from me."

Alexander smiled. "Thanks man, but we did just eat. I'm sure there are others in greater need."

"I was homeless myself for a while. I know it's hard, but keep surviving and moving forward. I used to be addicted to heroin. Things got really bad, but I change my life around. The day I decided to change, I had passed out high behind a dumpster. When I woke, I got up and went straight to the mayor to challenge him. They even wrote a news article about it." He showed them a picture of the article.

"That's great, man!" Alexander said enthusiastically.

"The bible says the meek shall inherit the Earth; that the lowest of the lows will rise up. That means you guys. God has a plan for us; we just have to keep pushing on and open our hearts to God. Since we're talking, would you guys mind watching a video?"

Alexander replied again. "Sure, man."

The older man waved the younger over. He dismounted and removed a small laptop out of a bag. When he opened the lid, a video already ready to play flashed on the screen. The young man knelt before Alexander and Lucas, holding the laptop, so both could see. He clicked play.

After a brief intro, a man appeared sitting at a table in a room covered with signs and slogans. They listen to the man speak of conspiracies against God by the government and corporations actively in progress. The most striking point, at least to Lucas, was the mention of a chip designed to be injected subdermally somewhere on the body. This chip would hold all of a person's information. The man emphasized the precarious financial situation that puts us all in. "*They* could simply turn off the chip and take everything away from you!" He assured that the implementation of the chip would lead to a new slavery and further straying from God.

The man never explained the details of the agenda of those responsible for the chip, but he vehemently condemned it as evil and a great act against God. He said the chip will start dispensing to the people the following year. Somewhere, the man also mentioned the failure of the U.S. dollar by the end of the year. Alexander and Lucas became confused under the onslaught of accusations. The message became jumbled. Then, the video ended.

"What I just showed you is very real. *I know*. These are dangerous times, and the world is on the brink of collapse. Now, more than ever, we need to get close with God." The older man paused as another man thirty feet down the road to their right waved. He waved back and gestured he would speak to the other man when he finished with Alexander and Lucas. "Sorry, I can't go anywhere without someone recognizing me and wanting to talk."

"You guys need to make sure you are reading the bible and connecting with people who can help support you." He reached back into his pocket and removed two business cards. Then, he handed one to each of them. "This place is a great place to help you get your lives together and to guide you towards God."

Lucas examined the card. It was cheaply made but served its purpose. Text stood out from a cloudy, blue sky with the sun's rays emanating from the bottom right hand corner. The card displayed the name of a church, its address, and other contact information.

"God's duty calls. We have to go help more people. Hang in there, guys and don't forget, now, is the most important time to connect with God." With that, the two men returned to their bikes and mounted. "Stay safe." They peddled off into the direction the other man had headed.

Lucas stood and walked over to the public trashcan nearby. He threw the card into it and returned. "We can never become like that." He said sharply. "We have failed completely when we reach that point."

Alexander laughed. "You got that right, man!"

"I just hope we can find a way to express our ideas in a sane way, but I'm not sure anyone will think we are sane."

"It's whatever, man. We just express how we can and let humanity decide what to do."

Lucas' phone vibrated. He had forgotten it there in his pocket. His father messaged "I am here." A grimness covered Lucas' face, but instantly, a determination took its place. "Well, it's time for me to go. My dad awaits us in the parking lot."

They stood once again, and gathered their things. Alexander discarded the empty jug into the as they passed the trash can. Then, they crossed the street, heading to the parking lot next to Alexander's home. Still, very few people wandered where they walked. Only one woman crossed their path. She walked with great haste in the direction opposite of them. Lucas saw something terrible in her eyes, and thought he heard a stifled sob when she passed behind.

When they reached the intersection before the road became the bridge, a train made its way past them. After it rolled by, they crossed to their left and then to their right. In a parking space adjacent to the border where parking lot ended and sidewalk began, the beige SUV waited. Lucas led Alexander towards it.

The driver's door opened, and Lucas' father emerged with an anxious smile. "I'm glad you are safe, Lucas." He, then, opened the trunk for Lucas and helped him load his things. After closing the trunk, Lucas hugged his father. "Thanks, dad."

Alexander placed his backpack on the sidewalk as Lucas loaded his, and now, walked over to shake Lucas' father's hand. "Good to see you again, sir."

"Dad, can you give us a moment? I'll join you in the car." His father agreed and got back in the vehicle. Lucas led Alexander back to the sidewalk next to Alexander's belongings. "This is it, man."

"Yup." Alexander smiled. "We will meet again, man. No doubt about it." Lucas' shoulders slumped, and his head struggled to keep itself up. "Hey, man! Be the best you can be, and the next time we meet, infinity will be ours."

Lucas met Alexander's eyes and smiled. He hugged him and then walked to the passenger's door. He entered and slammed the door. The engine rumbled with a start, and the SUV pulled out of the parking space and headed to the lot's exit. Alexander, already encumbered with the weight of his backpack, walked towards the exit Lucas and his father, now, turned on to the road from. As he watched Lucas drive away, the passenger window lowered, and Lucas stuck his head and arm out, waving whole heartedly. Alexander grinned and waved back.

EPILOGUE

Three books sprawled across his desk: *Plato's Republic*, *Making the Social World*, and *The Philosophy of Social Ecology*. Other books were stacked on the edge, and more were scattered on the floor. In the middle of his desk, a notebook lay open, and its visible page displayed sporadic clusters of notes and diagrams. On top of the notebook, a black pen rested at a slant. Lucas rolled his chair back to his desk and flipped through his notebook sending his pen rolling to the side. Then, he stood and continued marking up his whiteboard, adding to the large concept map already occupying most of the board.

Lucas stepped back and took a sip of his coffee. "Damn! This is difficult."

Suddenly, Lucas straightened as a familiar feeling returned with a precise thought. He put down his coffee cup and began packing his books and notebook into a black, nylon laptop bag. The bag bulged as he zipped it closed. He placed the strap across his chest, grabbed his keys, and hurried to his car.

The drive lasted approximately thirty minutes. Plenty of time for him to rest his mind and enjoy his favorite music. He found a parking space on a neighborhood road roughly three blocks from his favorite coffee shop. When he entered, he felt relieved there was not a line. He did not like waiting here. He only came here for a purpose he never wished to delay. He ordered a coffee and prepared it to his liking.

He found a table on the patio with a bench on one side and two chairs on the other. Hardly anyone sat outside. *Odd for such a nice day, and that breeze feels great.* After setting down his coffee cup, he unpacked his notebook, leaving his bag open on the bench next to him, so his books remained easily accessible. He flipped his notebook to a blank page, and at the top he wrote **Optimal Civilizational Design**. He stared at that blank page and sipped his coffee. Then, he picked up his pen, but before it could touch paper something stopped him. A familiar voice.

"I told you I would see you again!" Lucas looked up to find a beautiful girl with jet black hair and vibrant green eyes smiling at him. She sat across from him and reached her hand out as though she meant to shake his hand, but when he brought his hand to hers, she merely grasped on tightly. "My name is Jasmine."

www.ingramcontent.com/pod-product-compliance
Lightning Source LLC
Chambersburg PA
CBHW070332130626

46556CB00007B/2817